Fearless Warriors

Drew Hayden Taylor

Talonbooks 1998

Copyright © 1998 Drew Hayden Taylor
Published with the assistance of the Canada Council.

Talonbooks
#104—3100 Production Way
Burnaby, British Columbia, Canada V5A 4R4

Typeset in New Baskerville and Gill Sans and printed and bound in
Canada by Hignell Printing.

First Printing: August 1998

Talonbooks are distributed in Canada by General Distribution Services,
325 Humber College Blvd., Toronto, Ontario, Canada M9W 7C3;
Tel.: (416) 213-1919; Fax: (416) 213-1917.

Talonbooks are distributed in the U.S.A. by General Distribution
Services Inc., 85 Rock River Drive, Suite 202, Buffalo, New York, U.S.A.
14207-2170; Tel.: 1-800-805-1083; Fax: 1-800-481-6207.

Versions of these stories were originally published:
"Strawberries" and "Girl Who Loved Her Horses" in *Nativebeat
Magazine;* "Fearless Warriors" in *Callaloo;* "Someday" in *The Globe and
Mail;* "The Man Who Didn't Exist" in the anthology *Shade of Spring;*
"Ice Screams" in the anthology *Gatherings,* Vol. 3

Canadian Cataloguing in Publication Data

Taylor, Drew Hayden, 1962-
  Fearless Warriors

ISBN 0-88922-395-5

I. Title.
PS8589.A885F42 1998   C813'.54   C98-190720-5
PR9199.3.T35F42 1998

Acknowledgements

Fearless Warriors is a collection of twelve stories which have their origins in many different places, and with many different inspirations. Sometimes the stories began with one simple image or concept etched in my consciousness; other times the whole tale came completely from my subconscious. Storytelling, in my opinion, should always be a mysterious process, otherwise, there goes much of the fun. If we know where the stories come from, then the journey to where they end might seem a little less magical.

However, there are many people who are directly and indirectly responsible for inspiring these humble little yarns and credit should be given where it is definitely due. My special thanks to the following: David Johnson, Julia Taylor, Larry Lewis, Danielle Kappele, Dan David, various members of my family, and Dawn T. Maracle (who's a story in herself).

And my heartiest and most sincere thank you to all the little girls who draw horses on their walls, the boys struggling to avoid the ditches of society, the ark builders with dreams, the people who don't exist but really do, and the true fearless warriors of the world. Someday I hope to be one.

Ch'meegwetch.

Contents

The Circle of Death

The big dip in the road, the kind that leaves your stomach dangling around your ears, was the geographical road sign telling me and my sister we were now crossing into Japland. I never liked this part of the Reserve. Nobody really did. I guess that's why not too many people lived there.

The land in the area consisted primarily of a ground moraine, meaning it was made up of sand, rocks, clay and everything else useless to any long-term settlement. Only scrub brush, big pine and cedar trees, and just about every bug known to man populated the region, thanks to the swamp that framed the eastern half of the section. It was not a pretty place—most people avoided it if they could. But thanks to my sister Angela, and her job, I wasn't that lucky.

This rugged little plot of land the Federal government kindly gave to my people over a hundred years ago only because they didn't want it. It was christened Japland decades ago by some of our war veterans who thought the land was rough and undesirable enough to hide Japanese holdouts from W.W.2. There was also an unsubstantiated theory that the mosquitoes in the area were big enough to be mistaken for Japanese holdouts, but that has yet to be proven. Driving down the dirt road, looking at the hot, baked rock, I had better hopes for any such unfortunate Asians.

This was the kind of land good religious pioneers travelled across the Atlantic to tame and settle, feeling that the difficulty of the soil and the harshness of the land was rightful penance being doled out by God. They accepted it meekly. I've never been able to figure out white people.

The dirt road we were on was the only access into the area, except for a few trails cut out of the bush for ATVs and snowmobiles. This was the only reason anybody ever came into this area anymore.

"Look!" I pointed out a deer that was running across the road. "I didn't think there were any deer up this way."

"Mmmm...." Angela's mind was focused on the clipboard in front of her, as she busily scratched out a line she had only just scribbled down three minutes ago.

"What's another word for 'art'? I've used the word three times already."

I thought for a moment. "Crafts?"

"Used it." She snapped her fingers like she always did when trying to drag a word from her memory. Evidently it works for her.

"Creations. Fabulous creations. That's good." Again she quickly scribbled it down. My sister is proud of two things in her life: the fact that she's a vegetarian in a society where meat is a serious addiction; and that she considers herself an artist. Not an artist in the conventional sense, but in a more practical one, or so she says.

Angela makes quaint little things that tourists like to buy. She's developed somewhat of a reputation for her willow chairs—solid constructions made from laced willow saplings. Nice to look at, a bitch to sit in, but rustic enough for tourists to buy by the dozen. That and various other bric-a-brac "creations" gave my sister a purpose in life.

This little industry of hers was so successful, by her standards anyway, that she was now trying to organize an arts and crafts festival for the village. Over the first long weekend in August, she wanted all the local artists to put up booths at the community centre so that the tourists could come in and buy all the knick knacks their hearts desired.

Most of the stuff my sister makes, as well as that of the other "artists" she's contacted, is typical of the rural roadside things that can be found anywhere in North America. There's nothing particularly Native about them, so I was worried that the tourists who might drive all the way into the Otter Lake Reserve for this, expecting culturally-appropriate arts and crafts, might be a little disappointed. But Angela, my beloved and obviously determined sister, would hear nothing of it. Instead, she'd even invited some of the few non-Native residents of the village to participate.

"Other than the financial benefits of the festival, think of the community value. It will bring the village together." Somehow row after row of hand-made fishing plugs and tie dye t-shirts was going to unify the village. But hey, who knows? I'd seen lesser things tear it apart.

So, the First Annual Otter Lake Arts and Crafts Festival, coordinated by Angela, had brought us out here to Japland in search of artists. One artist in particular.

"There it is," she pointed. It was the old Marlowe house, a century-old farm house—a monument to a tragically failed experiment and faith.

I pulled into the overgrown driveway, two tire ruts barely peeking out of the weeds and grasses. Leaning against the house I saw the bike Allan Martin rode. He was a familiar sight riding into the village store, his bike looking older than he did. Allan was one of the few white people living full-time on the Reserve, by himself. A bit of a hermit and an oddball, everybody thought. He'd have to be, to live in the Marlowe house.

My mother told me that, when she was a kid, nobody ever went near the Marlowe place. And the fact that it was all the way out here in Japland wasn't the only reason why. Her grandparents had recounted a local legend to her about the Marlowe family, a Calvinist lot that had tried to scratch a living out of this land too long ago for people to remember exactly when. It seems the Marlowe family could produce plenty of kids—there were seven of them in the end—but not enough of anything else to eat or sell for food. According to rumour, weakened by hunger and malnutrition, they all eventually died, one by one, of tuberculosis in that house.

The house remained empty for over sixty years, getting older, darker, becoming part of local legend. Eventually it became an island of grey in a sea of green and rock. Whatever could be said about their dreams, the Marlowes sure knew how to build a sturdy house. Except for a certain weather-beaten appearance, it still looked solid.

Even during the Depression, when things were really harsh, the idea of putting new life or a new family into that tainted house was never entertained in the village. As my mother said: "The house was born of misery, and will die of misery."

Then, sometime in the late sixties (my mother says it was '69 but Dad swears it was the spring of '70) Allan Martin showed up. They said he had long hair, longer than most of the Indians in the village, and a backpack with the American flag on it. Usually the only Americans we used to get were fishermen or hunters, and he didn't look like either.

One way or another, nobody's quite sure, Allan Martin sort of ended up at the Marlowe house and had been there ever since. Nobody really owns the Marlowe place, nobody really cares, so nobody took any notice of Allan's residency on the Reserve. He kept to himself, making a living from various wood-based arts and crafts he'd sell to tourist shops in town, and never bothered anybody.

As we got out of the car, all we could hear was a million buzzing insects, some crows cawing and the creak of the only remaining barn door on the Marlowe farm. It waved back and forth in the slight breeze. Other than that, the place looked silent. Except maybe for the odd ghost still haunting the place. Or the ones I could imagine.

"Thanks for bringing me, Andy. I really appreciate it. Better safe than sorry."

"I'm sure he's harmless. Besides, he always looks like he weighs about what I eat in a day." Angela had been a little nervous about visiting Allan Martin, all alone, way out here in the bush. Eccentrics aren't called eccentrics for nothing. So I'm out here playing big brother, even though she's older than I am.

"Have you ever talked to him?" She said as she closed the car door.

"Once, when I worked that summer at the store. I waited on him. That was about it. Got some groceries, paid for them, put them on the back of his bike and pedalled off. No more than twenty words, I'd guess."

"Look." Now it was my sister's turn to point. I followed her lead and looked off towards the barn, about a hundred feet behind the house. There, spread out on the lawn, was an army of flat wood cut-outs of people and animals. Almost all were three or four feet tall, and about an inch thick; a cowboy with a cigarette leaning against nothing, a cow with a calf, bears, and so on. There seemed to be over a dozen or so, their paint drying in the sun. These peculiar lawn ornaments were one of Allan's specialties. Low cost, easy to make, cute and adorable. A sure-fire tourist gimmick.

"I bet these would go like hotcakes at the festival."

I couldn't believe people spent money on these things.

"We just gotta get him in the festival. We just gotta." My sister had found her calling. "Think he's home?"

I nodded towards his bike. Unless he was out playing in the swamp, he had to be home. "He's probably inside. Want me to knock on the door?"

"I can take it from here. You stay by the car."

"Out here, in the hot sun?!"

"Yes, out here. He might be shy. You know artistic types."

My eyes travelled to the wood cut-out of a woman's large behind in flowered bloomers, bending over, her rump obscuring the rest of her body. That was art to my sister.

Feeling the stillness of the summer air, and seeing the open windows of the Marlowe house, there's no way Allan Martin couldn't know we were standing outside. The noise of the tires on gravel, the growl of an engine badly in need of a tune up, and the slamming of two car doors could not be ignored. He knew we were there.

Angela approached the two-storey grey house, showed me two crossed fingers, then knocked loudly on the door. The crickets roared in the silence of our waiting. Angela looked puzzled.

"Try again," I said.

She knocked again, harder this time. The summer sounds

broke as a dog suddenly started to bark, rapidly, continuously. It sounded quite close, but came from behind the barn. My sister and I were exchanging curious glances when the door in front of her swung open. It took her by surprise and she stepped back a pace. The brightness of the sun made the door-frame seem like an entrance into night. I could see Angela squint into the doorway, trying to make out the person there.

"Uh, hello, Mr. Martin. Is that you?"

As if agitated by Angela's voice, the barking increased.

"Shut up before I come and shut you up" came a loud voice from the door.

Angela stepped back another step. But the barking stopped. Allan Martin stepped forward, into the light. "Not you, the dog. Stupid dog doesn't know when to shut up. Who are you?"

Both my sister and I looked him over. While he'd lived on the Reserve longer than we'd been alive, neither of us had ever seen him up this close for this long, at least not since that time at the store ten years ago.

He still had the long hair, held back by a bandanna soaked in sweat. He looked to be somewhere this side of fifty, with a wiriness that made him look fit, if not a little anaemic. His plaid shirt had the arms cut off and his jeans were worn. No shoes.

Angela put her hand forward. "Hi, I'm Angela Stone."

He looked at her, then over at me.

"That's my brother Andy."

I waved, forcing a smile. He did neither.

"Okay, Angela and brother Andy. You're obviously Indian, from the village. Am I being kicked off, after all these years?"

Angela faked a nervous laugh. "No, nothing like that. I actually want to talk with you about your art."

For the first time, Allan Martin showed an emotional response. Puzzlement flickered across his face. "My art? What art?"

"Your...carvings." Angela beamed as she waved toward the drying figures.

Allan blinked a few times. "Those things?! Those pieces of shit? Art?!"

"I see you're your own worst critic. That's all right, so am I. I mean my own worst critic, not yours. Anyway, I'm putting together an art festival of sorts and I'm very familiar with your work. So I was thinking...." Angela went into her spiel, which I'd heard perhaps half a dozen times this week already. I watched her get more animated. All the while Allan listened, not knowing what to make of her.

After a few minutes, Angela wiped her brow somewhat exaggeratedly. "It's really kind of hot out here, do you mind if we went inside to discuss this? So this is the Marlowe house. You'd be surprised the things I've heard about this place. I've even heard it's haunted...." Angela disappeared into the portal of darkness, leaving a surprised Allan Martin standing in the doorway, still puzzled. He'd just been Angela-cized.

Angela's voice boomed out from the interior. "Uh Mr. Martin, as I was saying...."

"Ah, your brother..." he said, still trying to gather his thoughts.

"Oh, don't worry about him, he's...claustrophobic anyways. He'll be fine. Now, the festival...."

I'm not actually claustrophobic, but my sister was on a roll. Pulled in by the vortex of her pitch, Allan Martin was drawn back into what had once been the safety of his home. He shut the door behind him but Angela's voice could still be heard pouring out through the windows.

"Everybody from the community will be involved. It will be bigger than the Pow Wow."

I lasted about ten minutes sitting in the car with the radio playing. I could feel my underwear beginning to melt. We had brought no water or anything cool to drink, since I hadn't expected to be banished to the car on one of the hottest days of the summer. Feeling the dire need for shade, I headed for the barn. The long building threw a wide shadow of inviting darkness. I even spotted a lawn chair near the far end of the shade.

Along the way were the dozen or so wood cut-outs Allan had placed outside to dry. In their own way they seemed kind of precious, I guess. I had a vision of every lawn in suburbia being covered with these things, and the owners chuckling to themselves at how cute their lawns now looked. Still, it was better than the '78 Ford that sat on my uncle's front lawn.

As I made my way around what looked suspiciously like a teepee, my foot hit a baby bear ornament and knocked it over. Not wanting it to look like I had manhandled the "art" and risk the wrath of my sister, I tried to right it. That's when I heard the growling—a deep throaty growling that would make a dog lover break out in a cold sweat. And there, just around the corner of the barn, was the source of the ominous rumbling, about ten or twelve feet away.

It was a big dog, mostly mongrel with a lot of shepherd and mostly in him. He was still growling, looking at me with brown eyes. He was in a sitting position, head slightly cocked to the left, watching me closely. And, luckily, he was chained. Thank God he was chained. Reserve life has taught me there's nothing worse than a dog with an attitude.

"Hi dog."

His response—a loud and vicious barking. It was so forceful I could almost feel his hot breath from ten feet away. I stepped back, tripping over the fat lady in bloomers.

"Shut up, you stupid dog!"

The voice from the house made the dog whine. Immediately, the dog lay down, his head resting between his paws, his eyes never leaving me.

Sitting there in the grass, surrounded by two-dimensional figures, I faced the animal. I wasn't afraid, just wary. A minor expanse of flattened grass separated us, but we watched each other.

The animal had a leather collar which was chained to what looked like a long-dead tree. Evidently, the years of friction from the chain around the tree had worn away its bark, killing it. Its dried branches hovered over the scene, giving no shade. A few feet from the tree was a home-made dog house, with a faded green roof. In front of it were some beat-up melmac pots used to feed the dog.

But the most startling feature was this: surrounded by forests and fields of vibrant greens, yellows, and pinks, nothing within an eight-foot radius of the tree was living. It was as if somebody had drawn a perfect circle around the dead tree, and then coloured everything within its boundaries brown or black.

Evidently, the dog had been there a long time, and as he had paced his small domain, he had ground under, dug up, or worn away all the grass, plants or bushes within his perimeter. Just at the edge of the chain line, the grass tried to invade the dog's space by a very perceptible line of growth.

It was a circle of death. Only the bleached, weather-worn roof of his dog house showed any sign of colour.

Now most dogs—and I've had a bunch of them—you can read immediately. The tail wagging, the set of the ears, the body posture, all give you a sense of how the dog is feeling. But with this dog you couldn't tell. It was almost like it didn't know how to respond. I had the sad feeling this 16-foot world was the only world it had known, and the man in the house was the only contact it had with another life form. And that probably consisted of a thirty-second feeding once a day. It just lay there, head on paws, eyes watching me. Not a twitch, not even a growl anymore. Whatever emotion or passion that had been in the earlier barking was now somewhere else.

On reflection it must have been an interesting scene, a chained dog, in a circle of dirt, looking at a man, sitting amidst a forest of cartoon like characters, who was looking back.

Most people who chain their dogs do it to keep them from running into traffic, which doesn't seem like a tough problem out here. Or perhaps because they are vicious and potentially dangerous. While this dog had a good voice for barking, it didn't strike me as a threatening animal.

Neither of us moved for the longest time. Eventually, I couldn't help but view his world with a morbid fascination.

Sure I felt sorry for the poor creature, but it wasn't my dog, it wasn't my house, the guy wasn't even a member of my village. I was just a visitor. That's what I kept telling myself until I heard the voice of my sister bellowing out across the farmyard. It was time to go home.

Leaving the dog behind me, for the first time I noticed the lushness of the summer grass and trees off in the distance, the vibrant green colour of the world around this farm. I had left the circle of death.

Angela was waiting by the car. Allan was standing in his doorway.

She was surprised to see me coming from the barn. "What were you doing back there?"

I answered by addressing Allan. "Nice dog."

"Thanks. Eats enough."

I guess when you're a bored dog, what else are you going to do.

On the drive home, Angela rattled on about Allan Martin and her conversation. I guess she had struck paydirt. He was interested, but as my sister so modestly put it, it took some fine negotiating and convincing.

"Did you know he was American?" My sister said suddenly.

"No I didn't."

"Yeah, he's one of them draft dodgers. Fled the States to avoid going to the that war in Korea."

"I think you mean Vietnam."

"Yeah, somewhere down there. That's why he's here. His family knew some fishermen who'd spent some time up here. Only place he'd heard of. Took off in the middle of the night and was here in two days of hitchhiking. Funny, but I'd never considered Otter Lake a place to run to. Been here ever since he says."

We were getting close to where I had spotted the deer earlier but there was no sign this time. "Does he know he can go back now? There's some sort of amnesty or something been declared a while ago. He can't get into trouble anymore." Angela shrugged. "I don't know but I kinda get the impression he doesn't want to go home. Says he hasn't written or gotten a letter in over twenty years. Doesn't have a phone. I don't think he cares. Sad, really."

"How'd you get all this out of him?"

"I just told him that we don't have many white people living on the Reserve all by themselves. So I asked him how he got here."

"That's it?"

"That and a photograph of him with his two brothers when he was young. The brothers were in army outfits, the kind Americans wear. I sort of made the connection. You know, he was kinda cute back in the sixties. Anyway, a few well-placed questions, some flattery about his work, and his history is mine."

She paused for a moment.

"I think he's lonely. He doesn't seem to have anybody."

"He has a dog," I ventured.

"Ah yes, man's best friend."

Two days later she told me she was going back to Japland to see Mr. Allan Martin. The Festival was two weeks away and she needed to talk with him about his booth and how many pieces he was going to display. Only this time she said she didn't need me to ride shotgun.

"He's okay. He's harmless. Besides, he's so skinny I could probably take him."

But I wanted to go.

"Why? I had to practically kick your butt into the car last time."

"It's a nice drive." A lame excuse but I gave it as much conviction as I could.

This time Allan Martin was waiting in his doorway as we got out of the car. He even acknowledged me with a scant nod.

Angela shook hands with him, before turning to me. "You want to come in with us? Get out of the heat?"

I shook my head. "I'm fine out here. You do your business." I gave them a polite smile, and in return got a confused stare before she and Allen disappeared into the Marlowe house.

She was right, it was another hot day, and the fact that I was wearing my jean jacket over my t-shirt on such a humid day probably didn't help my case. She knew me well enough to know something was up.

Once they were safely inside, I made my way past what looked like a wooden image of a buffalo, to the corner of the barn.

The last time I was here, the wind had been blowing slightly from the south, so therefore I hadn't noticed it. Today, there was practically no wind and it hit me as I got closer to my new friend. The smell. The dog looked to be about middle age, approximately five to nine years old. And if he had been chained all that time, with no bath, and sitting in five to nine years worth of dog shit, imagine the smell. No wonder the dog house was behind the barn. Allan had put it here on purpose, no doubt.

Breathing through my mouth, taking shallow breaths, and hoping my sense of smell would get used to it helped a little.

This time, the dog didn't bark. He was lying in the scant shade of the dog house, tongue hanging out of his mouth, staring at me again. It was as if he was expecting me.

I took my place on the grass in front of him and returned his gaze. I couldn't tell if he recognized me—his brown eyes didn't really convey much. I wondered if my eyes communicated anything to him.

Judging by his panting, and the sweat soaking into my shirt, the temperature was rising. I took off my jacket and reached into the inside pockets. The last time I was here, I noticed Allan fed his dog those kind of inexpensive, anonymous, dry, round pellets that passed for dog food, and it probably tasted as appetizing as it looked.

As I unwrapped the package, I saw the dog's ears shoot up. For the first time I saw interest wash across his face. Almost immediately, he moved from a lying position into a sitting stance, cocking his head as I pulled two large pork chops out of the styrofoam container. His tongue dripping wet for a different reason this time, he inched his body forward.

I tossed one chop, then the other into the circle of death. They both landed a few inches from his feet, little clouds of dust swirling up around them. After a brief sniff, he grabbed the first one and tried to swallow it whole but the bone made it difficult. Instead he wrestled it in half, using one paw to hold it down as his jaws ripped and pulled. The bone he crushed in his jaws. He made equally short work of the remaining one.

His tongue flicked out, washing his whole face, savouring every tiny particle he could find. I wondered if I had made a mistake. There are a few rules on the Reserve: never sleep with another person's partner, and never feed another man's dog. Both might get to like it. It's a good thing Allan Martin wasn't married too.

I don't know why I felt the need to buy groceries for a dog I barely knew. I had scarcely enough money to feed myself, let alone another man's pet. But something about this animal, his life, or lack of it, alerted me to the occasional need for human kindness.

I didn't know if I'd ever be out here again, and I didn't know how Allan would react. I didn't even know if I'd remember the dog next week, but I had done my little bit to make the world a better place. Maybe it would ease the feeling of guilt I'd had since I first saw the dog, a feeling I didn't understand, but couldn't get rid of.

After licking clean the paw that had held the chop, the dog gave me one final glance, then retreated to the relative cool of the dog house shade. We resumed our inspection of each other. Then, surprisingly, after a few minutes of watching me, and no doubt noticing there were no more delectables being thrown his way, he grew tired of my presence.

One of his paws began to scratch at the dirt. Gradually this became an increasingly important act to him. Driven, he rose to his feet and started digging manically, spraying dirt and dead grass out from under him. I could hear him whining in frustration. Then he stopped and sat down again, ignoring completely the five-inch deep hole he had made.

The circle of death was full of holes, scattered at random intervals throughout the dog's sixteen foot kingdom. That's all the dog had, or could do. His was a lifetime of digging holes and then, just as quickly, losing interest.

Once he snapped at an errant fly that buzzed too close. Mostly he'd lay down. His eyes lingered on me, then they closed. In a scant 15 minutes, I had just witnessed the entire life of this creature. This was all it knew, all it would ever know. And I realized that no amount of pork chops would increase its quality of life. Not as long as it remained in that circle, with that chain around its neck.

I sat there for a while, feeling the sad hopelessness of the dog creep into my soul. Despite an occasionally wayward childhood, the years have revealed what appears to be a conscience. As I sat by that circle, I learned just how annoying a conscience can be.

"Andy, where are you?" My sister's voice brought me out of my daze. I looked at my watch, realizing we'd been there about forty-five minutes.

I could see the two of them, standing by the car. They both seemed surprised to see me approach from the barn.

"Just looking at some of his...whatever you call them. The wood things."

My sister looked pleased. "We've decided to call them Pinnochios. Get it? little people and animals made out of wood."

"Cute" I answered.

"We thought so."

Allan looked uncomfortable. "It was your sister's idea."

Somehow I knew that.

Angela shook Allan's hand. "I'll be back on the weekend to pick up your Pinnochios. We'll set them up at the community centre that afternoon and be ready for customers Saturday morning. Okay?"

"Sure, I guess."

Angela gave him her best smile. "Oh, it'll be fun. Don't worry. Alright, Andy, I've got things to do. Let's motor."

Allan Martin waved after us, as my car dug up the weedy driveway. I was still feeling the effects of my visit with the dog. My sister must have noticed it because, in the middle of one of her monologues about life and the art and crafts world, she stopped.

"What were you doing by the barn?"

"Looking at those things you want to sell."

"They're in front of the barn."

"I thought there might have been more in the back."

"Were there?"

"No," I paused. "Just the dog."

Angela eased back in her seat, once again comfortable. "Oh yeah, he told me about his dog."

"He's got it chained behind the barn. It doesn't look happy."

"Poor thing."

"Do you know if it has a name?"

Angela thought for a moment. "No, he never mentioned it. Just refers to it as 'the dog.'"

"What did he say about the dog?"

"Not much, just that he's always tried to do a Pinnochio about a dog, his dog to be specific, but it never came out properly. Looked too silly, or the proportions were all wrong. Kind of ridiculous when you think about it. You'd think doing a dog, especially when you have a model right there in front of you, would be the easiest thing in the world. But I guess not. Instead he does buffalos, bears, cowboys...."

"Maybe it's too close to him. Maybe he needs distance."

Angela shrugged. "Maybe."

"Did he say anything else?"

My sister was quiet for a moment. "His two brothers are dead. You know, the ones I told you about that were in the picture."

"He told you this?"

"Uh huh. I asked him if his family ever came up to visit him. He got kinda quiet, then said his brothers died in Vietnam. Both of them. Seems they all were supposed to enlist together but Allan didn't want to, chickened out he says, so they did it without him. They were killed about a year after he came up to Canada. Poor guy, he couldn't even go home for the funerals because he'd be arrested."

I was trying to process all this information. Even eccentrics have a deeper, darker story. That's usually what makes them eccentrics. "This is all kind of personal to be telling someone you just met."

"He's definitely lonely. His mother's dead and he and his father haven't spoken in years. I think he blames himself."

We were quiet for the rest of the trip back to civilization, both lost in our own thoughts. I began to wonder how what happened to Allan Martin could screw up a life. Maybe if something like that happened to me, I'd end up in the woods, on an Indian Reserve in another country, carving fake animals and people out of wood, with a dog chained to a dead tree.

During the next few days, it occurred to me that I'd never noticed how many dogs there were on the Reserve, all of them running free, barking, chasing cars. Until now, I'd always been annoyed, screaming at the animals to not jump on me, not to pee on my car, and to get off the road. Now I watched with wonder as one dog chased a squirrel across a friend's front lawn. It was so caught up in the chase that the dog practically followed the squirrel half-way up a pine tree before the laws of gravity made their appearance.

Friday came and, for reasons that were mine, I offered to help Angela load up Allan Martin's "art" for her festival. This time she was glad to have the help. That and the fact my pickup truck would be better than her minivan.

All the way there she babbled on about the Festival—the promotional work she and her friends had spent the last month working on, all the local radio stations that had been running ads, and our one television station that was due to make an appearance at the festival. It was no longer just a community event. Angela had the knick-knack equivalent of Olympic fever. It wasn't a pretty sight. My mind, however, was on other things. But Angela was oblivious. She was giving this festival the enthusiasm reserved for the Second Coming, and she was John the Baptist.

For the third time in a week, we pulled into the Marlowe driveway. Beside the front door of the house was a neat stack of what looked like two dozen of the so-called Pinnochios, waiting to be loaded. Allan emerged from the darkness of his house, drying his hands with an old rag.

He threw the rag back inside the house. "You two always travel everywhere together?"

We looked at each other. "When we have to," my sister replied.

Allan shrugged and put his hand on the pile of cut-outs. "I have twenty here, think that will be enough?"

My sister's eyes lit up. "I hope not but it will do for now. Do you have a cheque ready for the fee for your stand?"

"I only work in cash. Makes life easier. I have your money inside. That was forty bucks, right?"

Angela nodded and followed him in the house. As soon as they were gone, I moved towards the age-old barn. There were no Pinnochios drying on the grass this time. The trampled grass was reflecting the sun.

A wind was blowing towards me, so I could smell my destination from a hundred feet away. I rounded the corner of the barn to find the dog peeing against the dead tree. As he finished, he trotted towards me, but was jolted back by the pull on his chain.

I reached into my coat pocket. Instantly he was salivating at the possibility of another treat. Instead, I pulled out a large hunting knife, one I'd had for about ten years, since the first time I went hunting. The dog looked disappointed, puzzled, even a little worried as I stepped across the green line into the circle of death.

The animal backed up a bit, not knowing what to do. He whined, let out a small bark. His chain was wrapped around the dog house, so he couldn't move freely. I took this chance to close in on the poor creature.

For the past week I had carried this dog with me, in my mind, my dreams, my consciousness. He would not leave me and I could not put him down. It occurred to me that the only way I would be free of the pitiful image that stayed with me constantly, would be to physically free the vision itself. No more circle of death.

Muttering words of hopeful pacification, I advanced on the animal, murmuring, pleading, talking gibberish in the hopes of gaining its confidence. I focused on the leather collar it wore, and I knew my knife would slice through it quicker than my wish to forget the dark circle I was in.

The dog could go no further, and the collar was straining under the dog's efforts. I saw my opportunity and I grabbed the chain near the buckle with my left hand and concentrated on the spot in the collar where I would cut the animal free.

Faster than I thought possible, the dog turned and bit me, hard, on the arm. In reflex I let go of the knife as the animal darted underneath me, throwing me off balance. I landed on my left arm with a second eruption of pain. The dog retreated to the dead tree. Before long, it had started to growl at me again. I knew I'd risk further, potentially worse injury if I tried to free it again. Instead, I grabbed my knife, and taking off my jacket, examined my arm. Blood oozed lightly from four specific puncture wounds, and about another half dozen fiery red dots slowly began to welt up. I wrapped my jacket around my arm and quickly ushered myself out of that ring of failure.

I bandaged my wound by the car, doing what I could with some band aids and an old bottle of vodka I had forgotten under the seat. As I put my jacket back on, I felt a peculiar sense of failure, of not being able to do a good deed through no fault of my own. I didn't know what my next move would be. The slamming of Allan Martin's front door drove me from my contemplation. My sister was coming towards me in a mood I had not seen in recent months.

"Get in." She was short and terse. I obeyed. "Let's go home." Again I obeyed and we were soon roaring down the only road in Japland.

Now I was in the difficult position of determining if I should ask, or wait for her to volunteer the information. Always an onerous decision.

Luckily I was saved the burden. "He's not well. That man needs serious help."

"Allan Martin? Why? What did he do?"

"You wouldn't believe it. The man's nuts."

"Could you be a little more specific?"

She looked at me, and there was anger in her eyes. Serious anger. "You wouldn't believe me."

She turned quiet again. I was just about to press the point when the gates flew open.

"We were sitting there at his kitchen table, drinking coffee as he was rummaging around in his cupboards for his can of money. He keeps all his money in an old coffee can. Hey I can accept that. Nothing too weird about that. Mom used to keep her money in the bottom drawer of her dresser, remember that? Then he starts asking me questions about you and me, about our relationship as brother and sister. I knew something was up but I couldn't put my finger on it."

"What did he want to know?"

"Whether or not I would die for you? Or you would for me? I tried to change the subject but it always came back to that. He kept insisting, asking, like he had to know or he'd die."

Then it occurred to me. "His brothers?"

"That's what I thought. And I thought, 'hey, this is a job for a counsellor, not me.' So I tried to get out of the situation but he asked me if I thought he was responsible for what happened to his brothers. If he ran out on them by coming to Canada. He thinks he killed them."

"Oh boy."

"I told him of course not, and that I didn't know him well enough to comment on any of this stuff anyways. That's when he started getting angry. He started accusing me of blaming him for what he did. Both of us in fact. He thinks that's why you never came in the house. You had condemned him and didn't want anything to do with him. And he started swearing that he did what he thought was best, the war was wrong, all this sixties shit, he wasn't responsible for his brothers dying in Vietnam."

"Maybe he should listen to himself."

Angela looked out the window. The dandelions had long since turned to white puffs of fuzz, which floated on the breeze. On first glance, it looked like it was snowing.

"He started crying as I got up to leave. I think their names were Robert and Bruce. Those were the two names he was calling, over and over and over again. Should I tell somebody about this? You know, to help him? After all, he is a lonely old man."

I thought for a moment. "This is a little out of the way of our Health clinic. Who would know what to do?"

"I don't know." She noticed the blood stains on my jean jacket. "What happened to you?"

"Nothing, just a scratch. It'll go away."

Angela was silent for a moment. "Do you think I should have stayed?"

I floored the gas pedal as we entered the dip in the road, signalling we were crossing the boundary and leaving Japland.

"Nah, not everyone wants to be helped."

Girl Who Loved Her Horses

Mom was kind of strange, and as a result she attracted other strange people. Every Indian Reserve in Canada has its share of strange individuals, just like any other town, but Mom sort of collected them like my sister's room collects dust bunnies.

And it was through one of Mom's peculiarities that I met Danielle, so many years ago. As a way of encouraging us kids to expand and develop our artistic nature, Mom set aside part of her beloved kitchen as a private art school. Near the back door, beside our antiquated refrigerator, was what she called "The Everything Wall." To eleven-year-old children, reality was what you made it, and mother understood that.

It was just a strip of wall, about three feet high and four feet long, just underneath where the wall paper started. It was painted white, and near the baseboard there was always a package of pencil crayons. Our job, and that of pretty well every kid in the village, was to keep "The Everything Wall" stocked with people, places and things. There was a never-ending stream of kids in our kitchen, all anxious to do the once forbidden but now legal act of drawing on kitchen walls. And every Monday she would get my father to paint it white again. Tuesday belonged to my sister and me. That was our day, and our day alone to draw the first images on that sacred virgin white wall. The other village kids could do what they wanted the rest of the week.

That's how we met Danielle. By "we" I mean William and I. William, not Billy or Willy as he always stressed, and I were best friends way back then. Nothing happened in the Reserve that we didn't know about, participate in or deny knowing anything about. It sort of set the stage for William's later election as Chief.

To us, Danielle was kind of strange. But it was nothing an

eleven-year-old could put his finger on. She was quiet, and seemed to be one of those characters you see in the comics with a little cloud over her head. Nobody ever paid much attention to her, she would just come and go. She was from across the railroad tracks in the non-status community. But we all went to the same school.

I think I'd seen her around for about two years before we'd ever talked. And even then it was only because I'd knocked her down once accidentally when William was chasing me. Then it was a simple "sorry" and I was gone.

That's why it was such a surprise to see her walk, however timidly, in through our kitchen door. William, my sister and I were playing our own version of crazy eights while Mom puttered around the kitchen doing odd things but never managing to organize anything. Danielle stood there at the door, her shadow falling across the sparsely decorated "Everything Wall" (it was early in the week). I think she was as frightened as we were surprised. We'd never seen her anywhere outside of school, and none of us knew what to say or how to react. Then, as always, Mom took charge. I think it was the little lost kitten look that emanated from Danielle that attracted our Mother.

"Well, hello there. I don't believe I've seen you in this house before."

"She's from across the tracks, Mom. Her name is Danielle."

Her maternal instincts in full blossom, Mom knelt down to her. Danielle looked so tiny and frightened, even we felt some inkling of sympathy for her, and you know how cliquish eleven-year-olds can be.

"Danielle. What a pretty name. And what can we do for you, Danielle?"

Danielle stood there, all four feet two inches of her. To us it didn't sound like that difficult a question, but it looked like Danielle was struggling with some eternal query of life. William snickered rudely, foreshadowing why he would not be Chief for very long. Finally Danielle, her eyes almost welling up with tears, looked to her right at "The Everything Wall".

Her voice sounded like someone had stepped on a mouse. "I heard that kids could come here and draw."

Mom stood beside us, a warming smile on her face. "I thought so. Well, it took you long enough to come and visit." This was true. "The Everything Wall" had been in existence for over three months by then, and every kid in the village who could hold a pencil and create a thought (and a few who couldn't) had muddied the floors of our kitchen.

Mom reached over and took a handful of pencil crayons from the package on the counter. "Danielle, who are your parents?" One of Mom's secret rules said: "In order to find out about the child, find out about the parents." Mom knew most people in the village and quite a few outside, too.

Danielle shifted from one foot to another uneasily. "My mother's name is Elsie Fiddler," she paused uncomfortably, "I don't have a father." Mom paused, and my sister and I noticed this. Evidently, she knew this Elsie Fiddler, and what she knew wasn't too good.

She handed the crayons to Danielle, studying her intently. At first it looked like Danielle was going to run, but she held her ground. Something in her wanted to draw.

To my sister and me, this amounted to a personal insult. It was Tuesday, we had sole right to "The Everything Wall." Even William stayed clear of it on this day. Unwilling to accept such indignities in our own house, we started to raise a protest. The protest remained lodged in our throats when Mom gave us her patented glare. It was a look that combined several different messages in one simple glance: "I'm your mother," "Don't mess with me," "Have some compassion," "I make the rules here" and a plethora of other statements. To this day I haven't mastered it, but I think it only comes with having children. They must teach it at the hospital.

With a slight mumble that might have been a "thank you," she took the pencils and knelt before the wall. Mom backed off and poured herself a cup of coffee. She smiled as Danielle squinted at the wall and made her first tentative marks. But, as always, there was housework to be done and no one but her to do it. My fourteen-year-old sister, as a political statement (or so she says) refused to do housework on principle. "These are the '80s, Mom. I will not become a prisoner to the house." She was quite emphatic about the whole thing, but I suspected that she was just lazy. The only woman I've ever known who got tired just going to the bathroom.

The rest of us watched for a moment before we got caught up in our card game. After a while, we forgot that Danielle was even there—that's how much noise she made, just the occasional squeak of a pencil crayon on a wall.

About thirty minutes passed before my mother came back into the kitchen and inquired about the game. I was losing as usual. Back then I sort of suspected that William cheated— little did I realize that later this would become a major factor in his demotion to ex-Chief. Watergate had nothing on him. I confessed that I was losing and waited for a soothing phrase or caress, which mothers are supposed to give. There was no reply, which was odd for my mother.

Mom was standing over us, staring at the forgotten Danielle, her body hiding the wall. I kicked my sister and nodded towards Mom, her back still to us. "Mom?" I said, a little puzzled by her behaviour.

She turned to us, with a look of amazement that I'd never seen before on her face. It was a look so few of us get in this world anymore. Below her, in front of Danielle who was putting the finishing touches on it, was the head and neck of a horse. But not just any horse. It was like no horse I had ever seen before, nor had my mother, my sister or my friends. Glowing with colour and energy, it covered a third of the wall. It seemed to radiate everything that Danielle, its creator, wasn't. The mane flowed in the breeze like flames from a bonfire. The neck was solid and muscular, something that had never seen weakness, and the eyes, those eyes flashed freedom and exhilaration. They surveyed a free prairie and a horizon to run to. The picture was breathtaking, not because

30

a ten-year-old had drawn it, but because it was a horse every human being on the planet wanted but could never have. Yet Danielle had captured it in her own way.

After adding a few touches to the mane, in just the right places, she calmly handed what remained of the pencil crayons to my mother, who took them silently, her eyes never leaving the horse that seemed to stare back. Danielle uttered another polite "thank you" and was gone out the door. We all were left to stare for what seemed an eternity at that amazing horse. My mother knelt and touched the horse's neck, never uttering a word.

That Monday, my mother refused to let my father paint it over. My sister and I had to agree—we never got tired of looking at the power of that animal. Our father argued that we shouldn't play favourites. If we saved one painting, what would all the other kids say? Mom didn't listen or care, and threatened to shave my father bald when he went to sleep if he touched that painting. We children, while feeling no particular fondness for Danielle, quickly offered to let Dad paint over our drawings to show it didn't bother us. Overcome by superior odds, Dad had to agree, though I secretly believe he, too, held a special fondness for that image.

So there it stayed. All the other kids were equally amazed. "Danielle did this?" was the common question. The following Tuesday she showed up again, at about the same time. Only this time she had a bit more of an eager expression, and almost a smile. Mom was overjoyed with her arrival and proudly showed Danielle the untouched picture.

Danielle stared at it, the look of eagerness and anticipation slowly washing from her face. She only uttered "it's still here."

"Yes dear, it was too beautiful to paint over. I thought we'd save it."

Evidently this was not in Danielle's plans. She suddenly went back to the Danielle we knew before, like a snail retreating into its shell. Mom couldn't understand it— she had expected Danielle to be flattered. Instead, there stood a small, deflated little girl.

"But I was told you paint it over so we can draw some more." It was then Mom realized her mistake.

For Danielle, the joy wasn't so much in having the finished project, it was the drawing of the horse that fascinated her. She wanted the horse to be painted over so she could draw it again, and again and again. It was sort of some childlike Zen thing I suppose.

That night, Mom again managed the impossible. She got Dad to whip out his paintbrush one day after he'd already painted most of "The Everything Wall," and miss his favourite wrestling show in the process. The wall was again pristine white.

The next day at school my sister and I tracked down Danielle as Mother had asked. We were all curious to see if she could recreate that memorable image of the horse. We told her it had been painted over. Standing there in the hallway, struggling to look into our faces, she nodded, "oh, okay then." She turned and ran off to her class.

"What a weird bird she is," replied my sister. I just shrugged and went on with my life.

I kind of got the feeling Mom expected her to show up that afternoon after school. This so-called "weird bird" and her perfect horse had definitely made an impression on our family. Every time a figure came along the road in front of our house, my mom would casually look out to see who it was. It wasn't until the following Tuesday that Danielle made another appearance.

Again she stood at the door, barely making a noise as she opened it and closed it behind her. She smiled at us faintly, and my mother smiled back. "You know where the pencils are, Danielle, and the wall."

With scarcely more than a "yes, Ma'am," Danielle was once again in front of "The Everything Wall." Only this time, she had an audience. My mother, my sister, William and myself never once stood up or moved, afraid it would destroy her concentration, although I doubt anything short of a nuclear holocaust would have bothered her. She ignored us all. We sat there and watched her for forty-five minutes and saw the birth of a horse. It was the same horse, exactly, stroke for stroke. It slowly took shape, a few broad lines gradually forming something wonderful. We were amazed. Even William, who has a snarky comment for everything, didn't dare say a word. In the end, Danielle stood back, checked over her work, and smiled her small smile.

"Thank you", was again all she said as she left. I don't remember if we replied. We were still in awe of what that little girl had created. The same magnificent creature we saw last week was there again in front of us. Our eyes traced every line, and drank in the picture.

Every Tuesday for the next year saw Danielle on her knees in our kitchen. It didn't matter what the weather was like outside, or what was happening in the village, she was there. Gradually the thrill of seeing her create wore off, but not the effects of the final image. Before school, going out to play, taking the garbage out, every time we went past "The Everything Wall" we would stop, even for a second, and admire "The Stallion," as we grew to call it. Sometimes the colour changed, and maybe a slight change in the direction of the mane, but "The Stallion" itself remained virtually unchanged for that year.

Once, I think in jealousy, William tried to make Danielle draw a dog, a simple dog. The always nervous Danielle capitulated and gave William something that loosely resembled a cross between an amoeba and a chicken. For Danielle it had to be a horse, that horse. "The Stallion" was part of her, and it gave her a chance to be something she really wasn't.

Sometime later William read a story, which in itself was unusual, about the Lakota warrior Crazy Horse. In the same book was an article about another great warrior cut from the same cloth, Man Afraid Of His Horses. William, with his peculiar sense of humour, decided to christen Danielle with a new name. Make her into some sort of a Warrioress for the meek, I guess.

"From now on we'll call her Girl Who Loved Her Horses. Everybody got that? That's her new name." Of course, after a few days, we all got bored with calling her such a long name and soon it petered out. I think Danielle was flattered by such a name, but of course she never said anything about it one way or another.

Then one day she stopped coming. Elsie Fiddler had met a man, got married and moved to the city, taking Danielle and "The Stallion" with her. Except for my Mom, we never grew particularly close to Danielle, no matter how much time she spent in our house. I felt we knew more about "The Stallion" than we did about her. In a bizarre way, we missed that flaming animal more that we missed Danielle. It was sad, actually. We never really heard from them again.

Thoughts and memories fade, and so does the need for an "Everything Wall." A few months after Danielle left, we slowly lost interest in expressing ourselves in such a childish way. It was also a pain to bend over to draw or get down on our knees. We had outgrown it in more ways than one.

We went on with our lives. High school came and went, then a year of college, and for me an engagement till she left me for a woman. William became one of the youngest chiefs ever elected, and also one of the youngest ever kicked out of office. He now runs a marina on the Reserve, plotting coups and revolutions. Mom and Dad separated, then got back together when Sis got sick. The doctor prescribed lots of exercise for her recovery, which to my sister was worse than cod liver oil.

It wasn't till I was 22 that I finally figured out what I wanted to do with my life, or the next little part of it anyway. There was an opening on my Reserve for a Special Constable, a police officer for the village. I kind of liked that idea, because I was always driving around running into deer and rabbits, but I never had a gun. I figured I could kill two birds with one stone, so I signed up.

Next I was sent to Toronto for some training. Evidently it's not kosher to just hand a gun over—you have to learn how to use it, not to mention all sorts of laws and things. After I got over the first couple of days of culture shock, I got to like Toronto. I'd go for all these long walks, trying to figure the place out. I'd match names of streets and places with names I'd heard on the radio or television.

On one of my walks I came to a place called lower Jarvis. It's not one of the healthier or wealthier places in Toronto, but I figured who's going to bother a six foot, two-inch, long-haired Indian. Probably another Indian, come to think of it. I walked by hookers, drunks, pushers and a variety of other strange people who made me wonder for the thousandth time how white people could possibly have beaten us.

I was down around Queen when this wino called to me. He was sitting against a building, almost hidden in the shadows. "Hey Buddy, got any spare change?" I thought people only said that in the movies, but, being the kind-hearted guy I am, I took a loonie out of my pocket and bent over to hand it to him. That's when I saw what he was leaning against. It was a large brown wall, with chunks missing from the edges. The nearby street lamp illuminated most of it, but you had to be in the right position to see it properly, it was so big.

There in front of me was an old friend, an old friend that had grown up big. The whole side of that wall, about nine feet high, was the head and neck of a horse, but not just any horse. "The Stallion" had returned.

The spray paint looked to be less than a year old, but the eyes said it was much older. Again it was the eyes that told me something. They were darker, sharper than I recalled. "The Stallion," I remembered, had eyes that gleamed exhilaration and freedom. Instead, this one yelled defiance and anger. It glared back at me, almost like it was daring me to do something. In a way, it frightened me. The eyes wouldn't let me go.

Something in the way they watched me said dark and unspeakable things had happened in the last eleven years. Like me, both "The Stallion" and Danielle had grown up. But unlike me, I had a feeling that they had been forced to.

The Boy in the Ditch

I never liked Paul Stone's office. It looked too...I guess too Department of Indian Affairs-ish, if you know what I mean. You could smell bureaucracy the minute you went in the door. The structure was built during the 60s by a sudden influx of money from the DIA and, as a result, it had that boring, anti-radical government feel to it. Standard government-issue walls for standard government-issue programs, most of them completely out of touch with Reserve-issue people. I know because I was one of them.

And then there was Paul's wall of knowledge. The ancient dry-wall was layered with rows and rows of Ministry-distributed posters warning Natives not to smoke, not to drink, to treat women with respect, to honour our Elders, and to stay in school. No matter who you were, just walking into that office made you feel guilty.

Paul was the drug and alcohol counsellor on our Reserve, the Otter Lake First Nations, a tiny blip in the Central Ontario we humorously refer to as our home and Native land.

Paul's office was an even tinier blip in the larger Otter Lake Band Administration Centre, located just off the main road. It was his responsibility to help the youth (and the adults if they requested it) keep a clean and sober lifestyle. He operated a youth group, ran the local A.A. meetings, and organized a number of events ranging from local regattas to dry dances.

But somewhere in his dedication to his job, his conviction had failed. A young boy, one we both knew, was dead. He had been found lying face up in a water-filled ditch back near the new subdivision. Nearby, the police had found a gas can, some plastic and, even though the boy had been submerged in six inches of water overnight, there was still the distinct aroma of gasoline coming off the body. That had been just a few days ago.

Incidents like this took the wind out of the usually outgoing Paul. "He was gas sniffing." As he spoke, I watched his eyes flow across the far wall of posters. He never looked at me.

"It happens." It was a stupid answer, I know, but it was the best I could come up with. I find it quite unnerving watching a man blame himself for a death he considers his fault.

Behind his desk, the corner of a poster had become unstuck. It flapped in the air-conditioned breeze. Paul reached over and pressed it strongly against the wall. A little too strongly, I thought. Again he spoke without looking at me. "Did you know him?"

"A little. He handled the balls and bats for out baseball team." He had lived right beside the baseball diamond so it was convenient for the team to store our equipment there. Other than that, he was the son of a second cousin. That was about all I knew about him. "His name was Wilson, right?"

He nodded. "Wilson Blackfish." He finally looked at me. "He was a good kid. I'm not just saying that because he's...dead. He really was a good kid, going places, smart in the head. He was only thirteen but he had good grades, solid family, no bad attitudes. He wasn't the type to waste it all on gas sniffing. This doesn't make sense. I just wish I knew what happened to him."

"Was it the gas that killed him?"

"Everybody's pretty sure but the cops want to be certain. The autopsy is being done today but the results won't be released for a couple of days. But let's face it, I don't think the results will be a suprise. While sniffing he was overcome by the fumes, passed out and rolled down into the ditch where he drowned."

"Maybe he had a seizure or something."

For the first time I saw emotion; I got the impression Paul wanted to throw his desk through the window. "Don't play games. I hate it when people play games about these things. It is what it is and that's the problem with this kind of abuse. People refuse to recognize it for what it is. It's called denial. I just can't understand why Wilson would do this to himself."

Paul continued to look at the wall covered in useless posters. "You going to the Wake tonight?"

"Of course. Is that why you wanted to talk to me?"

He took out a cigarette and lit it. The smoke curled around his head.

"No, I just want to put an end to this stupid, senseless behaviour. I'm trying to comprehend what would make a thirteen-year-old boy stick his head in a plastic bag and breathe gas fumes 'till he loses consciousness. I thought, maybe, if I talked to enough people who know him, I could piece it together and maybe figure things out."

Paul was a dedicated man, the product of his own misspent youth. He'd been there and come back a better man, and he wanted to make the trip as short and painless as possible for all the other travellers after him.

He played with the cigarette in his hand, evidence of his only remaining addiction. "I understand why people drink. Been there, felt it. Even some drugs I can grasp, but there just seems something so stupid, so useless about gas sniffing. There has to be a reason Wilson would do this."

"Wish I could help, Paul, but I barely knew him. Bought him a pop last month, that was about it. Sorry."

Paul put out his cigarette and stood to shake my hand. He forced a smile. "Thanks anyways. Hope I didn't drag you into my crazy mood."

"No problem. But Paul, sometimes things just happen. Just because. No rhyme, no reason, it just happenes. It doesn't make things any better, but unfortunately it's true."

I could tell Paul refused to believe me. Or maybe he was just too frightened to really listen. He couldn't grasp the concept of chaos, or the potential randomness of tragedy. "Truth or whatever you want to call this always has a reason. You throw a stone in the water, it makes ripples. You whack your knee, you get a bruise. A boy is found lying in a ditch, that's the effect, not the cause. That's my truth. I'll see you at the Wake."

Wilson's body had been found Tuesday morning, meaning the mourning process would start that night and run for three days. Tonight the Wake would be at the Blackfish residence. Tomorrow the viewing of the body would be at the Church. And finally, the funeral the day after.

That night, the lawn in front of the house of Wilson's parents, Harriet and Ward Blackfish, was lined with cars and trucks of all makes and descriptions. With the ground still wet from spring, the grass would bare the scars of Wilson's death for several years.

Inside, food was everywhere, and a million people forcing conversation, looking for a place to sit or at least put their plates down. The temperature soared with the sheer numbers of bodies. Wilson was a well-liked though innocuous kid, and so were his parents. Everybody felt obligated to show up.

I found Harriet, the shock of the event barely twenty-four hours old etched on her face, trying to make small talk, but with little success. She would muster small spurts of meaningless conversation, momentarily pretending to forget why everybody was there, then it would all come crashing back to her. Her voice faltered and her eyes moistened. Ward Blackfish, on the other hand, was standing in the corner, eating a piece of peach pie, looking very stern. He was not the type of man to show or take weakness lightly.

Harriet's sister Beatrice shoved a half-full plate into my stomach as she sat quickly beside the distressed woman, trying to comfort her. Harriet barely noticed.

"Why did he do this to us? Didn't he love us? Why didn't he say something?" Beatrice did what she could, but what could she do? Harriet continued to ask the same questions over and over again, more often to herself than the people around her.

"This isn't like him. No, not at all." She turned, speaking directly to me for the first time. "You should see the painting he gave me. Boys who give presents like that don't...do things like this. I mean that's not a normal present for a thirteen-year-old boy to give his mother for her birthday. But it showed he cared, doesn't it?"

I guess I had paid more attention to Paul's little lecture earlier in the day than I had intended to. I found myself asking, "What painting?"

Her eyes moist, she pointed vaguely to the back of the house where I knew, from snatches of conversation, that Wilson's room was located. "It's in...his room. He got his art teacher in school to draw it. Wilson gave it to me last month for my birthday. What am I gonna do with it? It doesn't even look like him. I told him I wanted a watch, that's all, just a simple watch, but...." At this point, her wall of strength fell with a flood of tears.

Concerned relatives whipped by me, surrounding Harriet with rows of comfort and murmuring platitudes, forcing me away towards the far side of the house.

Without really being conscious of it, I found myself standing in front of Wilson's door. And again, not really wanting to, my hand turned the door knob.

The indelicacy or just plain rudeness of entering the bedroom of a recently-deceased boy weighed heavily on my mind as the door opened, revealing the private world of Wilson Blackfish to me. I don't know what I expected, but the normalcy of the room, the averageness of the decor startled me. It was a teenage boy's bedroom. Music posters on the wall, some car and sports magazines scattered haphazardly on the floor, the bed wasn't even made.

It was very similar to the room I had as a boy. Eerily similar.

Peeking out from under the bed, rolled up into a small thin tube held together by an elastic band, was what looked like a painting. Everything my mother had taught me about invasion of privacy screamed how disrespectful this was but curiousity knows no mother. I picked up the work and slowly unrolled it.

It was like Harriet said. It was a painting. That's all, nothing special. Competent but hardly memorable. It was easy to recognize Wilson's smiling face in the odd swirl of impressionistic water colours. Personally I thought it was a great idea for a present, though not particularily well executed, but I guess Harriet had been brought up in a more austere time. Her pragmatism clashed with Wilson's inventiveness.

"What a waste of money." Ward stood in the doorway, looking at Wilson's smiling face in my hands.

"He paid his teacher to do this?"

"To do that? Nah, but he bought the paper and paints and God knows what else they use. He should have known his mother wouldn't want something like that. The boy wasn't thinking."

"I think it's kind of nice. Something different."

Ward took the painting from my hands, and held it for a moment as his thumb absent-mindedly rubbed up against the rough texture of the paper. You could tell there was a universe of thoughts milling behind Ward's stoic face. Then he quickly rolled it up into a tube again.

Tossing the painting back under the bed, he turned away intending to leave. But something made him stop, hand on the doorknob, back still to me.

"I don't want you to think wrongly about the boy's mother. It wasn't that Harriet didn't appreciate it, it just didn't fit. You know what I mean? It's like giving a fisherman a hunting rifle, or an alcoholic a salad. It just doesn't belong. We just like things to belong."

The door opened, flooding the small room with the sound of several dozen conversations as Ward rejoined the world outside that bedroom.

On the second day came the viewing of the body. The parking lot around the Church was full. I was standing outside with several of my cousins as they smoked, delaying the solemn event, when Harriet and Ward arrived. Our attempt at normal conversation trailed to an end as their car pulled up. Like an old-fashioned gentleman, Ward jumped out first, looking dapper in his dark suit, a startling change from his usual green work clothes. He opened Harriet's door, helping her out.

It didn't look like Harriet had gotten much sleep. She managed a weak smile at us as she and her husband walked by. Ward gave us all his customary single, quick nod before entering the Church.

"Who'd a thunk it, huh?" Kelly, my cousin on my mother's side, was the first to recover. "Little Willie, dead. You just never know, I guess."

"Little Willie?"

"Wilson. I used call him Little Willie to tease him. He hated it too, really bugged him. He was kinda serious. I'll miss the little guy."

Pete, Kelly's brother, lit up another cigarette. "Yeah, I remember you calling him that. He started crying once, he got so upset."

"Yeah, 'geez,' I told him, 'it's only a nickname.'"

Paul approached us, dressed in his standard D.I.A. suit. "Hey guys, sorry I'm late. Everybody in there?"

I nodded. "Any news about the autopsy?"

He shook his head. "They won't be releasing any information for a few days. It'll only confirm what we already know." He took a deep breath. "Well, I'm going in."

Pete and Kelly echoed each other's "Me too," and followed Paul into the Church. Much like last night in Wilson's room, I was left pondering the many images of Wilson, always coming back to the last one: a thirteen-year-old boy, found dead in a ditch, staring up into the sky. It was the image that was growing more difficult to lose.

Inside the Church the organ was playing, and people were lined up, side by side with family seated at the front. There was the odd whispering of muted conversations and not so subtle observations, and the usual sporadic coughs and sneezes. I took a seat on the left side, close to the aisle, while people filed by the body. Waiting my turn.

It came quickly, and with it a feeling of reluctance. I've never understood the viewing of the body but it is tradition and everybody knows how Native people like to hold on to tradition. Like something from *Fiddler On The Roof.*

Except for being unusually well dressed, Wilson looked the same as the last time I saw him. I did notice, though, that the corners of his mouth seemed to be frowning. In the picture he'd given his mother Little Willie had been smiling. Not anymore.

As usual, my imagination was working overtime. I thought I could barely, almost, smell just a hint of gasoline hovering over the casket. I know that Wilson had probably been washed, cleaned, and obviously groomed. There was no possible way I could smell that faint aroma. It must have been just my imagination.

The viewing lasted deep into the night. The next day came the funeral, scheduled for two o'clock. The casket was loaded into the hearse and was trailed by a procession of anybody who wanted to follow the long black vehicle, as it made its way a half mile down the road to the graveyard.

The sky was clear, a good day for a funeral. At first the walk behind the hearse, dressed in my dark respectable suit, wasn't too unpleasant. There were about a hundred of us walking behind Wilson. The rest of the mourners, those too old or just unwilling to walk, were following in a chain of cars and trucks.

I walked beside Warren Dieter, a teacher at the local high school in town where we all used to go. He'd been there as long as I could remember. All the Native students used to joke that he had lost a hair follicle for every student from Otter Lake he taught. He was now completely bald.

I hadn't talked to him in years, but he remembered me.

"You're Angela's younger brother, aren't you?"

"That's me." I shook his hand as we walked on.

He took a handkerchief out of his pocket and wiped the sweat from his shiny forehead. Dark suits and a hot day were not a good match.

"I taught Wilson, you know. God boy, a great help in the class. I thought he'd be smarter than this. Poor boy."

"He was a cousin," I replied.

"Everybody out here is a cousin." Mr. Dieter was right.

It was still another ten minutes or so to the graveyard at the pace we were travelling. I tried to make conversation, but what do you say to a teacher you never really cared for in the first place? "Boy, this sun is hot."

Again, wiping his forehead, he looked up at the sun. "It takes roughly about eight minutes for the light and heat from the sun to reach our little planet Earth. Over ninety million miles away." Did I mention he taught science?

"What you're feeling, the heat that is, is the infrared radiation, not to be confused with the ultra-violet radiation. It's a shorter wave length on the electro-magnetic spectrum."

"I remember. We went through this ten years ago."

He scratched his head, thinking. "Is that how long it's been? Time sure does pass. I used to teach Wilson, eh? Good student. Bright kid."

I stepped up my pace, uncomfortable at the awkwardness of the discussion. "I know. You told me already."

"He wanted to be an astronomer, Wilson did. Fascinated by cephoid variables, pulsars, binary systems, all the wonders in the heavens. Dreamed of it, he told me."

This view of Wilson was what I remembered of him. He had always had a dreamy quality. And I guess people who wanted to be astronomers needed it. I remembered he used to love going out on the family boat, anchoring a couple of hundred feet off the shore, then spending hours looking up at what I thought was the sky. But now I guess it was really the stars. Hell, everybody around here has done that at one point or another. Out on the lake, the stars look close enough to reach, and I suppose Wilson wanted to touch them.

I smiled at the memory. "Wilson probably would have made a great astronomer."

"No, he wouldn't have." Mr. Dieter made it sound so matter-of-fact.

"But if he liked that kind of stuff, and was smart...."

Mr. Dieter shook his head. "I think he got most of it from all those science-fiction shows. Astronomy is hard work, very hard. You have to be committed. Plus, Wilson's maths weren't good enough. They were okay, but he wouldn't have been able to grasp all the physics and trig necessary to be a half-decent astronomer."

"You told him this?"

"Definitely. I liked him. Thought he had a bright future ahead of him. In something he could understand and handle. Better to save him the heartbreak now, than have it complicate his future. I like to encourage my students, but I like to show them reality too. Let's face it, not a lot of want ads for astronomers. You have to be exceptional. How many great astronomers can come from the Otter Lake Reserve? We'll, we're almost there, eh?"

At the graveyard, Wilson was lowered into the ground, in the opposite direction of the sky he had found so inviting. On the way back to the church for the reception, everybody seemed more animated. More conversations, louder voices, a few more smiles and even some laughter. The downcast mood had been put to rest along with Wilson.

The next day, I found myself in Paul's office, seeking closure I guess. The corner of the poster that had proved difficult for Paul a few days earlier now held a gold-coloured tack. Paul was staring at it. The room stank of cigarettes.

"Well, what did the autopsy report say?" I hovered in the doorway.

Paul took a drag of his cigarette. "Just like we thought. They found water in the lungs. Wilson Blackfish was overcome by gasoline fumes, lost consciousness, fell into a water-filled ditch and drowned. That's the story. That's the end. And I hate it!"

He threw the cigarette at the poster, making it explode in a shower of sparks. Paul was still hurting, feeling powerless.

I felt the same, but for a different reason. "Paul, if it makes you feel any better, Wilson didn't drown."

Paul raised his head above his own impotence, confusion splayed across his face.

"Uh, yes he did. The report...."

I shook my head, too confident in my knowledge.

"He didn't drown. He suffocated."

Paul looked more confused. I closed the door behind me, letting him wrestle with what I'd told him. It was getting late and I wanted to get to the marina before it closed. The weather report had said the skies would be clear that night.

Strawberries

"So, what will we have next?" I asked.

We'd been asking each other that question for the last two hours and it still brought deep thought and even deeper study of the drink menu. As was our yearly ritual, Joby Snowball and I were blowing our first paycheck of the season on absolutely nothing worthwhile. It was a time-honoured tradition we loyally kept. I had just started a new job for the summer at the Band Office, occupying specifically the well-respected title of Day Camp and Regatta Coordinator for all the little ankle-biters of the village. It was work on the Reserve, therefore no income tax to worry about, and it was close to home so I could save even more money for my next year of college.

Joby's paycheck was different from mine. We had grown up together, played together, chased girls together, and even caught a few together, but in many ways we had drifted apart. I did the collegiate thing while he had remained on the Reserve being a working man, doing odd jobs, mostly seasonal things. During the winter he'd plow and sand the roads, put up storm windows, things like that, while I was off in the city eating food he'd never heard of. But every summer I'd come home, he'd still be there, and we'd try to pick up where we left off.

This summer, Joby was ground-keeping for both the baseball diamond and the cemetery—life and death, cheering and quiet, action and peace. In many ways, the contradictions in his job reflected our relationship.

That is how we found ourselves sitting at Charley's, an upscale bar in downtown Peterborough. I had gotten my first paycheck that day, not nearly enough money for looking after two dozen little Indians who evidently believed in human sacrifice. Meanwhile, Joby had received his the day before, and, despite tremendous temptation, it was still firmly lodged in his back pocket. Until today, that is.

When we were teenagers, we'd spend our first cheque of the season on movies, comics, toys, food and various other things of no great or lasting importance. And like clockwork, our mothers would chew us out for wasting our money, foolishly believing their lectures would have some lasting effect.

Gradually, as we got older, our tastes changed. The comic books evolved into other magazines of questionable quality. If our mothers had ever found out about some of the magazines we spent good money on, we would have received more than a lecture. But that was a long time ago.

"Well, what do you think?" It was Joby's turn to ask the famous question.

I couldn't decide. We were having a drinking contest. A sophisticated one of sorts. I was showing off, ordering a variety of interesting yet bizarre drinks I had learned about during my brief excursion into the equally interesting and bizarre Caucasian world. Joby on the other hand was matching me exotic drink for exotic drink, having watched many a soap opera and movie. We had just finished a Vodka Martini, shaken, not stirred. I believe Joby had picked that up in a movie for the same reason he referred to his pickup truck as his "Austin Martin."

We had been there two hours but we weren't drunk by any measure. Joby was a beer person through and through, and I still had an affinity for rye and coke, the mix I was weaned on. So with all these new liquors and liqueurs, we were taking it slow and carefully, as all scientists do with their experiments. So far we had also tried White Russians, Black Russians, Brandy Alexanders, Sea Breezes, Singapore Slings and Manhattans. We prided ourselves in "how international" we were being.

Now the ball was in my court. "How about a strawberry daiquiri? I hear they're pretty good."

Joby stiffened like I'd slapped him. "The hell they are. My

strawberry days are over. Pick another one."

"What do you got against strawberry daiquiris?"

He looked at me for a moment. I could tell he was remembering. Not the kind of memory that follows a story line or pattern, the sort you see in movies, but the kind that brings back a random series of emotions and experiences. Sort of like having a pail of water suddenly dumped on you when you heard the right word or saw the right image. Judging by the look on Joby's face, the water was cold.

"You were lucky," he said, "all through high school you got to work at the band office. Just ten minutes from home, air conditioning, and a chair to boot. You forget what I did all those summers."

Then I remembered. The fields.

"For three goddamned years I picked strawberries. I'd come home with my hands stained blood red, my back ready to break from bending over all day. A sixteen-year-old shouldn't have back problems, it ain't right. When I turned seventeen, I swore I'd never pick another strawberry in my life, or eat one, or look at one, or even think of one."

That's the way it used to be when we were young. Local strawberry farmers would send in these huge flat-bed trucks to our Reserve to pick up the Indian kids to pick strawberries. We used to be like those migrant workers except we weren't migrant. We lived on the edge of the fields.

The rookies would gorge themselves on the berries for about the first three days or so. But the novelty would soon wear off with the knowledge that, since you got paid by the pint, you were actually eating your salary. Picking strawberries was on the low end of the totem pole when it came to jobs. Most of my uncles and aunts, at one time or another, picked strawberries. They referred to it as "paying your dues." But by the time my and Joby's generation arrived, Pick Your Own Strawberries were coming into vogue for all the yuppies from the city, all that health and get back to nature stuff they like so much. So Joby was part of the last group of kids to be hired in our area to hit the fields.

"One time my sister had her room wallpapered with pictures of that toy character, I think her name was Strawberry Shortcake. I coulda killed her. There were strawberries all over her room," he was getting excited. "All over it. I think that was her way of making sure I never went into her room. I had nightmares for a week. Andrew, to this day, I've never eaten a strawberry or even touched one and I hope I never do. To me they're the Devil's own food. Now for God's sake, pick another drink."

Trying to be sympathetic (it's remarkably easy to be sympathetic in a bar), I ordered a grasshopper. We were quiet for the next little while, the spirit of our adventure having been spoiled by the berry from Hell. We tried to recapture the fun of our outing, but the moment had been lost to a bad memory. We had a few more drinks, then went our separate ways. As he walked away, I realized how much I missed the closeness we had shared as kids. No amount of this new age "male bonding" can ever come close to two fourteen-year-olds trying to convince our Day Camp counsellors to go skinny dipping with us. And I couldn't even swim.

It was two days later that I heard the news. There would be no more drinking contests, no more summer reunions, no more berry horror stories. Joby Snowball was dead. He'd been hit by a produce truck at the Farmer's Market just outside of Peterborough. His mother, Winnie, always used to send him in to do some early shopping for her.

The village went into shock. I went into shock. At a very important time in my life, he had been my best friend. Nothing could take that away from us. Life would go on for me, but not for Joby.

The wake was held two days later. I went to see my friend, lying there so peacefully, wearing the scarlet-coloured tie he always hated but occasionally had to wear. His head was framed in red satin. He looked healthier and wealthier dead than he ever did alive.

Afterwards, we all went to his mother's place. Everybody was meeting there and bringing food, something I could never understand since nobody at these things ever felt like eating. All I could find to bring was a bucket of chicken from you-know-where. Poor Winnie, she never slowed down for a minute. Playing the perfect hostess, she refused to let anybody help her as she put out dishes, set out the food, even washed the odd set of dirty dishes. My aunt said it was her way of dealing with the grief.

I looked across the table ladened with food. There were about thirty people in the house, and everybody had brought something edible, so the table was fairly sagging under the weight. Everywhere there was food of every possible description: casseroles, salads, chicken, even apple and, yes, strawberry pies.

I sometimes wonder about the irony of the universe, but, as my Grandmother would say, who am I to decide what's ironic? That's for God and English teachers to decide.

That night I ate my fill, somewhat guiltily enjoying the strawberry pie, but my perpetually dieting sister reassured me that food and guilt always go together. Pretty soon I left for home. I had to get up very early the next morning to fulfil an obligation and do my last favour for Joby.

Since Joby had looked after the cemetery, and then died, it left a problematic vacuum. But in my community it was considered an honour, albeit a sad honour, to be asked to dig a grave for a particular family member or friend. So, oddly enough, Joby had never dug an actual grave—for which he was very grateful. That is why I found myself at the grave site, shovel in hand, and a lead weight in my heart.

It took me a moment to psych myself up. This is not a thing one normally learns about in school. I'd dug many holes in my life, but none eight feet by four feet. But digging that hole, lifting shovel after shovel of heavy earth, gave me the opportunity to think about Joby, all the paychecks we had planned on cashing in the future, and all the fancy drinks there were left to discover. Something again made me think about the food at last night's Wake, and Joby's consuming hatred of strawberries. I thought about my grandmother too, and wondered if God had a sense of humour.

A little over three hours passed before I finished. Digging a grave in a ground moraine is a real pain; every six of seven inches there was a rock, sometimes a huge mother of a rock, sometimes a whole bunch of rocks fighting to get on your shovel. But I managed to pull it off, with only three pulled muscles, although I barely had enough time to get home for a shower and a change of clothes before the funeral. Joby had always hated suits and he was being buried in the only one he had ever owned, the one his mother had bought him for his high school graduation eight years before.

The funeral went well, as well as funerals can go. It was a good turnout—his mother appreciated all the extra mourners. The minister said some nice words about a boy who never went to Church. As Joby lay quietly in his coffin, I remembered that he was slightly claustrophobic, too.

It took me less then a third of the time to fill in the grave than it took me to dig it. The only company I had was the lonely sound of rocks and dirt hitting the wooden casket, and even that gradually disappeared. Before long I was patting the dirt down solidly but gently. I stood there for a moment, looking at the grave site, saying a quiet goodbye to my friend, and coming to a realization.

God did indeed have a sense of humour. As I turned to leave, I was careful not to step on some tiny white flowers, no bigger than a dime, which littered the area around the grave.

Wild strawberry season was just around the corner.

The Art of Knowing Better

The birds were quiet now. The last call of the crow and cry of the robin had disappeared with the setting sun. I could tell that the wind, which had died down during the early part of the evening, was picking up once more, rustling the trees and making the smaller ones bow down to the moon. Another evening in Otter Lake.

Outside my room, the summer insects buzzed and crawled across the window screen, trying to get at the light that burned above me. I turned it off. I wanted the quiet of this summer night, as I listened to the village wind down. Another day to be knocked off the calendar. The universal rituals that end all days around the world vary little, even in this small Ojibway community. Everything was finishing as it normally did.

On my bed in my mother's house, I lay there waiting for the next link in the unalterable chain of evenings that make up my Otter Lake life. Without it the day couldn't finish. Not officially, anyway.

Except he was late this evening. Not too late, but later than normal. Ever since I could remember, since we had moved into this house, even during the winter when the snow would muffle—but not quite completely hush—his footsteps, this would be the beginning of my morning and the end of my day. Tonight I wondered if maybe the wind was carrying away the familiar shuffle of his feet on the dirt road, that he might have already gone by, hidden by Mother Nature.

In the larger scale of life, the sound of this old man's footfalls wasn't all that important to me. I mean, I barely knew the man. But this was like the old clock my grandmother owned when we lived in the old house. Like old Tommy Hazel, it had its place. The clock was an ancient thing, ornately carved in a cheap and gaudy way. It sat on a mantle high above the livingroom and had to be wound twice a day with a funny-looking key. My grandmother would always curse that it kept losing eight minutes every twelve hours.

As a young child, I remember looking all through the house for those missing eight minutes, not knowing where they could have been lost. The more time the clock lost as the weeks and months passed, the more I knew was waiting to be found. Every time she turned that key, I was sure I could see eight tiny minutes fall from the old clock into a crack in the floorboards directly underneath.

And still it sat, looking down on us, ticking away loudly. As a kid, I always imagined I could see a face—not a pleasant one—peering out from the carved and shadowed wood. It was watching me, angry about those missing eight minutes getting away. At night I could hear its ticking echo through the house, bouncing off one wall and then another until it ended up on my bed: tick, tick, tick, tick, tick, tick, tick, tick. Then I would fall asleep.

When we moved to the new house, modern, with electricity, indoor plumbing and a television, the first thing I noticed was no more ticking. The house was silent except for a long-distant hum somewhere buried in the walls. Without the ticking from the angry clock, I couldn't sleep. I tossed and turned for three nights until I did sleep, however fitfully, from sheer exhaustion. It was months before the electrical humming would allow me to sleep soundly. Even then I would lie awake, consciously straining to hear the ticking.

I remembered asking my mother what had become of the clock. She had told me it was still over at the old house, still with my Grandmother. Probably still losing eight minutes every twelve hours.

I heard a stone being kicked and the tell-tale thuck of it hitting a tree. I hadn't missed him. He had officially ended this summer day. From behind the window screen, I saw him passing the house as he normally did; head hung low, eyes on the ground, shoulders slouched, his knees perpetually bent, like his legs could never make a full commitment to walk. His shiny hair was combed back in its usual style, vaguely reminiscent of a fifties' ducktail.

Old Tommy Hazel was at least sixty, but looked twice that age. So did his clothes. Every morning, as long as we'd been here in this house, he would make his way along the road into the village, usually to get drunk, if he wasn't drunk already. And every evening, his mission completed, he would retrace his steps back to his place of origin; somewhere in the northern part of the Reserve, which is largely swamp. The place has a Native name, but it's hard to spell and harder to pronounce, unless you've been born speaking the language. And the name's not really that translatable. It might be loosely interpreted as: "the kind of place white people like to explore for no practical reason except to say 'because it's there!'"

Old Tommy Hazel was a local legend, a mystery, verging on a bogeyman. Even though the man had lived in Otter Lake all his life and everybody knew him, nobody actually knew were he lived, other than the fact that it was deep in the swamp somewhere. And nobody really wanted to know, either. Except me.

I was curious. After watching this man walk by my house for the last twenty-odd years, I couldn't help wondering where his daily journey began and ended. I had no logical reason for wanting to see with my own eyes where he lay his head down at night. What little I'd seen of his life didn't interest me much. In my life, I'd said perhaps a hundred words to him. We were supposedly distantly related, but that's nothing. Everybody in Otter Lake is.

Still, the question of Old Tommy Hazel—where dawn found him every morning and where day left him every night—nagged me. Nagged me to the point where I would listen more intently than I should every morning as he walked by, and every night as he staggered home. I would imagine how long he had been walking. How winded were his sixty-year-old lungs? He was an old man, with an alcoholic's body; he couldn't walk that far. But then again, you can't always judge an alcoholic by the standards we apply to ourselves. My grandmother used to say that God loves fools and children, and that drunks could be classified as fools for the lifestyle they've chosen. It does, however, seem that drunks have a unique ability to survive what they do to their bodies, and whatever the fates decide to throw at them. I've heard about drunks falling asleep in snowbanks, getting hit by cars, falling off hills, committing numerous other atrocities against themselves, then getting up and walking away. No worse for wear.

Old Tommy Hazel had a home somewhere out in the swamp, and for no reason other than curiosity, stupidity, and perhaps a little of that "because it's there!" philosophy, I wanted to see it.

I slipped out of my bedroom and went to the back door, as I'd been waiting to do. I allowed him a few minutes' head start. I ran silent, I ran deep, as I exited the house on my mission. I didn't have to see him to follow him. He had a noisy, shuffling walk, as if the effort of lifting his boots more than an inch off the ground was a waste of time. I, on the other hand, in an effort to walk like a ghost through the forest, dug deep into my soul, determined to find that "inner-Indian" many in the White world think we automatically possess. I found myself dodging thorn branches, hanging vines, bushes that grabbed at me like one of those black holes scientists are always talking about. The further Old Tommy Hazel got into the swamp, the wetter my sneakers (and I use the term loosely) became. My "inner-Indian" was evidently on vacation.

But the marshy ground allowed me to drop back another hundred feet or so. Tracking became easier. The footprints from those big, industrial workboots he favoured left deep and unmistakable tracks in the soft, wet ground. They were easy to follow, sponge-like impressions slowly filling up with water, leaving behind oblong puddles through the bush. Even at this distance I could hear him huffing, his blood straining to turn the oxygen and alcohol into usable fuel for his trek through the swamp. Still he kept walking.

I trudged along behind him for about half an hour,

careful not to get too close or curse too loudly when my sneakers were sucked off my feet by the oozing mud. I was also aware of the growing darkness, and the emergence of night noises. The sun had set not that long ago, but the twilight that happens on lazy summer days always gives the impression that it will last longer than it really does. This is not good when you're in a swamp, a fair distance from home, in the dark, following the town drunk to God knows where. Puddles in the ground are hard to follow home by moonlight. In retrospect, the whole evening might not have been such a good idea. I should have known better.

So, lost in my increasing concern over my situation, I didn't notice that the thwuck, thwuck, thwuck sound of Old Tommy Hazel's big old work boots had stopped. Only the sounds of the night accompanied my heavy breathing. Suddenly realizing this, I held my breath and kneeled down behind a half-dead cedar tree. I immediately noticed two things: first, I could just barely make out Old Tommy Hazel's laboured breathing, now more calm, hovering somewhere to my right. Second, my right knee was wet from kneeling in a swamp.

The tell-tale sound and flare of a match being lit drew my attention to the old man's location. Just a couple of dozen feet ahead of me, beside what appeared to be a small lake. In actuality it was no more than a less-treed opening in the swamp around us.

As he lit his cigarette, I saw that he was sitting comfortably on a weathered log jammed into the fork of two trees growing side by side. The top of the log was shaved or hacked off into a level platform, making for a comfy bench.

The light went out, and he disappeared back into the growing gloom. He sat there, probably just looking out over the water, thinking his Old Tommy Hazel thoughts. As he thought, I kneeled, first on one knee, then the other, then back again, the fallen cedar offering me scant cover, even in the growing darkness.

I had long ago given up maintaining any semblance of

dryness, and accepted the growing dampness with resignation. Time passed and still he sat there.

I must have counted over a dozen cigarettes, with no signs of movement from Tommy. A lot of time had passed, but I had long since lost track of it. Instead, I found my attention and frustration turn towards the minute denizens of every swamp which were quickly becoming infatuated with me. I no longer heard Old Tommy Hazel's breathing. The only noise I was conscious of was the whining and buzzing of probably a thousand skimmag, better known as mosquitoes, all calling my name.

If I slapped at them like every fibre in my body was telling me to, I would certainly alert Old Tommy Hazel. If I let them bite me, I would look like I had chicken pox the next morning. The only solution was to move an available arm slowly, hoping to crush the little biters without generating enough sound to travel the thirty feet or so to the old man. Of course, half of them escaped before being crushed, leaving behind red polka dots. And my slow movements allowed a dozen others to land in the meantime. Evidently, my only recourse was not a viable one. The evening was not turning out the way I had anticipated.

With my body soggy on the lower half and itchy on the top half, I had had just about enough discomfort for one night and was more than willing to announce my presence to Old Man Hazel and the whole swamp, and to follow up that announcement with a speedy retreat home. Provided I could find the direction of home.

Swearing to myself in misery, I stood up, shaking my arms and head violently in an attempt to dislodge the mosquitoes from my body. It was then that I noticed Old Tommy Hazel standing in front of me. Actually, slouching in front of me would be a better description. He was watching me. And still more mosquitoes came.

But they didn't seem to be bothering him. By the light of the three-quarter moon, I couldn't see one flying insect on his tanned and lined face; his hands never moved to destroy a single annoying skimmag. It seemed that the pungent aroma emanating from him, an odour derived from a lifetime of drinking which seeped through his skin, appealed to the mosquitos even less than to me.

His eyes squinted in the dimness. Self-conscious, I could do little but squirm.

"Hi." What else does one say in such a situation?

He looked at me closer, then turned away without even a shrug, returning to his seat by the lake, silent as the image of the fading moon reflected in the water.

I saw the strike of a match. I guess meeting me in a swamp meant time for another cigarette. Studying the situation, debating in my mind, reaching a decision, I joined Old Tommy Hazel. He didn't look up. Just gazed out onto the open swamp. Over by the water there seemed to be more of a breeze, giving me a brief respite from the mosquitoes.

"I don't know if you know who I am but you walk by my house every day. Actually twice a day." Options for starting a conversation in a swamp can be limited.

Old Tommy Hazel switched the cigarette from his right hand to his left, and then reached into his coat pocket, bringing out what looked like an unopened mickey of rye. Not one of the more popular brands, either. With a surprisingly quick flick of his wrist, he broke the seal and unscrewed the cap. Raising it halfway to his mouth, he paused, and for the second time looked at me.

I don't know if it was the moonlight, but his eyes looked like they had a transparent film covering them. My grandmother used to say eyes like that were covered in memories. He raised up the freshly-opened bottle that smelled so similar to the old man himself, offering it to me. Realizing this was a potential test, I accepted the bottle and took a drink. Again, I should have known better. It burned. More than burned. I normally like Rye, but with a little coke and a lot of ice. And a better, smoother, more expensive brand. Trying not to cough, I handed it back, my eyes tearing.

He took the bottle and drained a good half of its contents,

his eyes never leaving the water, his hand never shaking. Old Tommy Hazel then offered it back to me, his saliva still wet on the bottle. Not caring about tests anymore, I declined.

"So, you live around here?" I actually sounded casual.

He looked up at the stars. "Time. I've lost track of the time." He spoke in Ojibway.

"It's a little after 10, I think." I answered in English since, as my mother and grandmother complain, my Ojibway is too rusty to be called conversational. But I could understand it well enough.

He shook his head. "No. How old am I?"

I blinked at him for a second, trying to make sure I understood what he said.

"How old are you? Is that what you asked?"

He nodded and finished off the last half of the rye, again without blinking an eye. With a grunt, he leaned back and tossed the bottle out into the water. It landed almost dead center in the small lake. The ripples patterned outwards, making the moon dance in front of us. Somewhere at the bottom of that tiny expanse of water, I wondered how big a pile of empty bottles there was.

I cleared my throat. "I think you're somewhere in your sixties. Maybe sixty-five. You don't know?"

His attention returned to his cigarette. "I forgot. You forget so much. Or try to. Or try not to. So much depends...." Silence. Even the mosquitoes were quiet. "So old," he added.

"You know something else? I could have been somebody. I wanted to. Had plans. Had dreams. Wanted a wife and children. Could have had them. Could have. But I don't. Sixty-five." His head leaned slightly to one side, the thoughts weighing too much.

In my travels I had discovered there are two types of drunks: the aggressive variety who are easy to identify, and the passive, emotional kind. The belligerent kind force their drunkenness onto the world, whether the world wants it or not. They are outgoing. The more placid drunk works in the opposite manner. They invite or welcome the world into their reality, often trying to fill a hole in their existence with whoever happens to be around. They smile, joke and sometimes cry.

One tends to view town drunks as caricatures, seldom as people with a history or a soul. It must have been a long time since Old Tommy Hazel had talked to anybody other than a liquor store clerk. Who was willing to listen? As it was, I was feeling uncomfortable. "Old To...I mean Mr. Hazel, sorry for...."

"It wasn't so wrong. I know it. The Bible makes exceptions. It wasn't wrong, was it?" For the third time he looked at me, searching for an answer I didn't know.

"I'm not sure...."

"It wasn't!" This time his voice was more insistent. Whatever was or wasn't wrong was the core of this man. Cheap amateur psychology would also suggest maybe this was at the root of his drinking, too. Some people are born drunks, others become them for a variety of reasons, most of which are listed in a million country songs. Old Tommy Hazel had a sign on him a mile wide that said this life was chosen for him, not embraced by choice.

"It wasn't." Softer this time. "Wasn't." Smaller, almost silent, his voice seemed to falter.

"Mr. Hazel, what wasn't so wrong?"

Out of nowhere, a coughing spasm hit the old man. He leaned over, his chest and body wracked by fits of deep coughing that didn't sound healthy. For three or four minutes he was plagued by continuous phlegmy upheavals which finally subsided. Staggering to his feet though still out of breath, he pushed me aside and continued his journey into the swamp. "It's late," I heard him mumble to himself. He quickly disappeared into the gloom, leaving me behind with as much of a mystery as before, perhaps even a bigger one.

On my long and confused journey home through the quagmire, I thought I heard a sudden splash far off in the direction I'd come from. I found myself hoping it wasn't Old Tommy Hazel.

The next morning and a bottle of calamine lotion later, I asked my mother about Old Tommy Hazel. She didn't know any more than I did about him, but she did have one important suggestion.

"Ask your grandmother. This was a much smaller place back then, and everybody of her generation grew up together. She can probably help you more than I'm able to." A good idea. One I decided to pursue.

My grandmother lived alone in the old house I grew up in. When I arrived, she was sitting out on the porch, watching the cars pass, an adored pastime of hers. She had always told me I was her favourite grandchild, but then again, she told that to my sister and about a dozen other cousins of mine. She was a very diplomatic grandmother.

She squinted when she saw me. I itched all over. "What happened to your face? Got a couple bites there. Out late last night, were ya?"

"Kind of. Just being stupid. Granny, what do you know about Old Tommy Hazel?"

"Old Tommy Hazel?!" My grandmother let out a short, throaty laugh. "Stupid things and Tommy Hazel go together. He's a drunk. What more do you need to know?"

"Where does he live?" I asked.

She looked at me. As best as I could tell, trying to figure me out. She took the most direct route. "What's it to you? You been talking to him? What did he say to you?"

I started to answer when I heard a sliver of my childhood coming from an open window just behind her. It was the familiar tick, tick, tick. I visit my grandmother quite frequently, but I'm always five years old when I hear that sound, or see that clock on that ledge looking down at me. And when I hear that ticking I have to fight to stay awake. Pavlov has nothing on that clock.

"I'm talking to you, boy," said my grandmother. I was awake again.

"Can't a guy just be curious?"

"Raccoons don't root in your garbage unless they smell

something. What are you smelling?"

I gave her my best exasperated look. She gave me a better one. I tried a different tack: "Nobody in the village knows where he lives. All anybody says is it's somewhere back in the swamp. I just want to know if he has a house back there or does he sleep in a tree or something. I'm not up to mischief or anything. I'm just curious. Mom thought you might know. That's all. Really!"

My grandmother was silent for a moment. Two cars went by and her eyes quickly scanned them. "You pick the weirdest things to get curious about. I mean, where Old Tommy Hazel spends his nights? You have too much time on your hands."

A large cloud passed overhead, plunging everything into shade. My grandmother's eyes returned to me.

"Did you know him? You two are about the same age, aren't you?"

She leaned back in her chair. "I knew Old Tommy Hazel way back, before you, your mother, even before I married your grandfather. Except he wasn't called Old Tommy Hazel then. Just Thomas Hazel. He was named after one of the Apostles. A good name for a good man." Another car went by but she never saw it. I'm not sure she saw me.

"But Grandma, you just said he was a loser"

"He was a good looking man back then. Tall, hard worker, even went to church. Sure wasn't the man you see today. Not by a long shot."

"Did something happen?"

She smiled. "I guess you could say that. For a while, a long time ago, we were bus'gems."

It took a moment for the translation and the reality of that sentence to filter into my consciousness. Bus'gem is an Ojibway word for boyfriend or girlfriend. The path to Old Tommy Hazel's home was taking me along a few unusual stops.

My reaction must have caught her eye because she gave one of those throaty little laughs of hers. "Don't look so surprised, you. When I was young, I was young!" She threw off the final word of that sentence with more enthusiasm than I'd seen from her in a long time. I tried to see her being "young!" The shawl and rocking chair didn't help.

"And Thomas Hazel was young too. I always thought we were a good match. He made me laugh, and I made him work harder than he ever did in his life. He was always buying me presents, you see. Always blamed his bad back on me. Like I held a gun to his head to make him work so hard." She laughed again, but it wasn't as joyful as it should have been.

"We'd been seeing each other for a couple of months when our fathers put a stop to it. Told us both we should know better. It wasn't right, they said. In fact, his father even called it evil."

I knew something was missing. "Called what 'evil?'"

She looked at the road again even though no cars were passing. "We were cousins. First cousins at that. They were right, we should have known better. It was wrong." After that she was silent. I sat there, trying to imagine Old Tommy Hazel as my potential grandfather, and me with two heads playing a banjo. It was all too odd for me.

My grandmother cleared her throat and continued. "I had always felt a little uncomfortable with the whole thing, but he said it didn't matter. Thomas said he knew it was right. Felt it, he said. It was even in the Bible in places, you know. As long as it had God's blessing. Adam and Eve's kids populated the whole world. And he was sure we had God's blessing. I thought that was a stretch but I was too fond of him to care."

I tried imagining that man I met in the swamp saying those things to my grandmother, but the two distinct images were having a problem connecting in my head.

"After we stopped seeing each other, our fathers went out of their way to make sure we never met up again, or spent time alone anymore, which was hard to do in a small village like this. I grew to accept the situation. Women are a lot more realistic about these things. But Thomas never did. Never. Some months later, I started to see your grandfather, and a year later we were married."

The clouds passed from in front of the sun, and the dazzling brightness of the summer day momentarily blinded me. Grandma closed her eyes and leaned back in her chair.

"I remember coming out of the church with your grandfather on our wedding day. All the people were there on the steps, throwing things and cheering. All those smiling happy faces. Except for Thomas. He was standing across the road, a little ways to the left. All alone, hands in his pockets. He was watching us. I tried not to look at him, but I could feel him staring at us. I almost tripped coming down those stairs, but your grandfather caught me. Once I righted myself, I forced myself to look up. Thomas had turned his back and was walking down the street, away from us. I think it was then and there that Thomas became Old Tommy Hazel. I don't think we've talked since. And I think that was the last time he was sober. At least that's the way it seems.

"It was two days later when I was going outside to fetch some water for my new husband's coffee. When I opened the door, I hit something." She pointed with her thumb through the open window in the direction of the tick, tick, tick I still heard. "It was a large clock, made of wood, that someone had left on our porch. There was no name, no wrapping, no clue of any kind. Just a big old clock."

"Old Tommy Hazel?" I asked.

She smiled a faint smile. "I think so. I don't have any proof, and he'd probably deny it, but I'm sure Tommy left it. He always liked to buy me gifts. I guess this was one last one. Sort of a reminder of different times, maybe. Or that he'd be waiting. And much like Old Tommy, it never worked properly since." She shook her head like she was shaking off cobwebs.

"All this talking to answer your silly question. I have no idea where he lives in the swamp. He moved out on his family soon after I got married. His family tried to help him, but he kept pretty much to himself. Can't help an alcoholic if he don't wanna be helped."

So that was it. I went looking for Old Tommy Hazel's home and instead found a story, a family link in fact, to how this man ended up living in that swamp. And my Grandmother was at the centre of it all.

"And you haven't talked to him since?"

"What's done is done. He's an old foolish drunk now. He didn't have to become that way. He could have gone on with his life, found another woman. Done something good in this world. Instead, he's Old Tommy Hazel. Ain't got no reason to talk to him."

Both her reasons no longer lived. Her father had long been dead, way before I was born. And my grandfather, her husband, had passed away a good seven years ago that winter.

"I know what you're thinking, boy, and no need for that. The past is the past, and there's no way to relive it unless you have one of them time machines I see in them movies you like. Lives aren't meant to be lived again. I'm too old to start walking backwards. Let it be. Besides, I've got better things to do than waste my time with an old foolish drunk."

"That's kind of harsh," I said. That didn't sound like my Grandmother—however the subtext did suggest to me a certain memory from high school: 'perhaps the lady doth protest too much.'

"It's true that I do feel sorry for the man, I don't deny that. The way Thomas spends his days is a disgrace and to be pitied. But he made his choice. I wish there was something I could do, but that was forty years ago. Our days together are long apart. If God wants me to talk to that man again, then let him tell me in his own way. He knows better than you or me. Now leave me be."

Before taking my exit, I excused myself to use my Grandmother's bathroom, her pride and joy since the renovations eleven years ago. As I entered her house, I heard the clock again. Its tick hadn't changed over the years, except maybe that it sounded more tired and worn. And the shelf seemed a bit lower now, or perhaps I was just a bit higher.

I couldn't help thinking of that clock as the time machine my grandmother had imagined earlier. And Old Tommy Hazel leaving it behind for her. Or, as my grandmother believed, it was God looking down on us all, remembering a forty-year-old relationship.

Several days later, my supply of Kraft Dinner was running dangerously low and I was on a weekly pilgrimage to the local village store to stock up. As chance would have it, I decided on that beautiful summer day to take the path through the woods. Most of my relatives believe that if a trip involves walking farther than the length of your driveway, you take the car. Luckily, I hadn't reached that stage in my adulthood yet.

The path cuts through a small abandoned quarry and then, for a few hundred feet, it runs along the edge of the swamp. Under my feet the ground was still spongy, making me conscious of the dampness that still lingered in my sneakers.

It wasn't long till I came to the part of the path where Old Tommy Hazel leaves the civilized part of our village for his nightly excursions into his unknown world.

As I expected, his bootprints had made their mark in the soft soil. Not that long ago it seemed, because the water was still leaking into the deep impressions. This in itself was unusual, for it was midday, long before and long after Old Tommy usually used the trail. The normal sequence of events had been broken.

That was only half of it. Running parallel to the bootprints were a pair of smaller shoe prints, barely two-thirds of Old Tommy Hazel's boot size. A couple of times the work boots had stopped and shifted position, as if to help somebody over a log, or a large puddle. They trailed along the swamp's edge, and finally turned east, disappearing into its centre.

God must have graciously decided to bless Otter Lake with a sign. Or perhaps it was that I had stopped on my way to the washroom at my grandmother's, and stuck my jackknife into the keyhole where my grandmother winds the clock. I jiggled the knife until I felt something snap deep in the mechanism. My grandmother must have tried to wind the clock later that same day, but I guess the time had just run out.

Or maybe it had something to do with the next morning when Old Tommy Hazel had been on his way into town.

Before he had had a chance to hit the liquor store, I waylaid him as he passed in front of my house. My mother was at work, so no one noticed the strange man I put in the shower, gave a clean pair of pants, underwear, t-shirt and shoes (which I'm hoping to get back some day). Nor would she have heard me tell the startlingly different, almost presentable man about a broken clock, an old lonely woman, a sign from God, and the concept of second chances. God knows it's hard to wipe away forty years of self abuse in one morning but I was willing to give it a chance.

I tried to do some mental calculations about those missing eight minutes every twelve hours. If those minutes were all added up over the last forty-odd years, all that time hidden under the floorboards and in the cracks in the walls, they would come to roughly six months or so. That's a lot of extra time she had coming to her. My grandmother may not have known better, but for the first time in a long while, I felt I did.

And maybe someday, if she finds the time or the interest, Grandma might just tell me where Thomas Hazel lives, way back in that old swamp.

Fearless Warriors

To put it mildly, the girls were not in a good mood. In fact, they were acting as cold as the wind buffeting our car as we drove home through the fall night. The two of them, Barb, my girlfriend, and Marie, William's, sat in the darkness of the back seat, fuming, barely saying a word as I drove and William tended to his rapidly swelling eye. And as usual, he had a big grin on his face. The girls might have been angry but William was cheerful enough for the two of them. Me, I long ago learned not to get involved when these two opposing forces met, which unfortunately was quite often. I just pointed our standard Res car in the direction of home and took care of the driving.

William repositioned the rear-view mirror to examine his new facial feature. "Ooh, that's a beaut. Mom's gonna kill me. Or at least blacken the other eye." That was William; an angry girlfriend in the back seat, a hell of a shiner and he still worried about his mother's reaction.

"Luckily, I was too fast for the guy. He gave me his best shot, and of course my shot was better." Even in pain he could brag.

"William, we're getting a little too old for this bar room brawling stuff. My fist hurts." And it did. William was far more the he-man type than I. It seems my duty in our friendship was to back him up and make sure he didn't get into too much trouble. And that's what I'd done tonight, or tried to, and that's why Barb was mad at me.

William winced as he touched his rapidly darkening eye, as if hoping he could rub the discolouration away. "Oh yeah, you were a lot of help. That second guy was practically on top of me before you decided to give a friend a hand."

"That's because that other guy was the bouncer and I don't

like mixing it up with bouncers. I don't like fighting period. Now we're barred from the place for life. Thanks a lot, William, I liked that bar."

"Oh, don't whine. We're Ojibway men, fearless warriors from a long line of fearless warriors."

"William, your father pours cement."

"Details. It's the spirit of the idea. We got a long history behind us. We weren't gonna let a couple of farmer boys tell us anything, now were we?"

I personally wouldn't have cared one bit if they had recited the American constitution, but William had a way of getting everything he wanted. And a few things he wasn't expecting, like his black eye.

"I just wanted a beer and a dance. That's all, William."

William flipped back the rear-view mirror as he chuckled, "well, you got a show too, and some exercise."

I just stared out into the dark strip of road that lay ahead of us. It was still fairly early as weekend evenings go, but as happens in the fall, the nights come quickly and can be very dark. It had been raining the last few days so there was no moon over us as our car cut through the slight fog that hugged the road.

I kept replaying the evening in my mind, trying to find some way of making an excuse and getting back into Barb's good graces. We had bumped into Steven Arnold, a guy we went to school with way back when, until William decided to drop out and pursue a career in anything he could get away with.

I could see the storm clouds brewing when Steven, quite good naturedly, made some comments about William's lack of education and whether he could spell "beer." In typical William fashion, he responded by telling Steven what he could do with that beer, as well as another comment I only caught a bit of—something about Steven's unusual fondness for cattle.

Not long afterwards Steven and William, in their tumble, had knocked off a record seventeen beers, twelve liquor drinks and God only knows how many bowls of popcorn. And I found myself with this bouncer in a headlock, trying to figure a way out of all this. It was then I noticed Marie and Barb in the corner, seething with embarrassment and anger. To tell you the truth, I would still rather face the bouncer.

As usual, William was oblivious to the condition of the ladies. "Do you think this eye makes me look more rugged, Marie?" There was no answer from the back, only the sound of wind whistling past the partially opened window. I silently prayed to myself that William would see the futility and possible danger of trying to strike up a conversation with them in their present condition.

But William twisted around in his seat, his one good eye showing irritation.

"Are you still mad at me? Get over it, Marie. It wasn't that bad."

My palms were sweating, making me grab the steering wheel harder. "I wouldn't if I were you." Again I found myself looking after William's well-being. At the age of twenty-five, it can get quite tiresome finding yourself babysitting someone your own age.

"Relax, Andrew, Marie still loves me, don't you sweetie?"

I risked a look in the rear-view mirror, knowing that, like William, I was playing with fire. But that's one good thing about being friends with someone like him. He may get you into trouble, but you can always count on him to take the brunt of the punishment and redirect unwanted attention away from more innocent people such as, mainly, me.

The back seat was too dark for me to make out anything, let alone the girls. There were no other cars on the road to provide auxiliary light. It reminded me of a horror story I'd read somewhere of a naïve and unsuspecting man driving with a huge, vicious monster hiding in the back seat. Now I know where he got the idea.

"Don't talk to us."

Those four short words from behind said it all for me, and I was perfectly content to heed them, but evidently they didn't say enough for William.

"Don't be like that. Come on, it's over. Forget about it. Don't make a big deal out of it. Right Andrew?"

There was only one thing I could say. "Keep me out of this."

"Thanks a lot, buddy."

"Hey, you started this evening, you finish it. I got problems of my own."

And unfortunately, there was William to my rescue, in his own particular style. "Oh leave him alone Barb, he didn't do anything wrong. Except date you." A small chuckle. That was William for you.

Suddenly, out of the darkness, Marie's face appeared between us as she confronted William.

"I know Andrew didn't do anything. As usual this is all your fault. What is it with you all the time? Always got something to prove, no matter what the costs."

"Yeah, okay, so things got a little out of hand." He pointed to his eye. "This will heal and it will all be forgotten. These things happen sometime. That's all."

At this point, Marie was practically shouting in William's face, making him slide sideways in his seat till his head was resting against the window.

"But it happens all the time. Something pisses you off and you decide to get all macho about it and ruin the evening for us. You've been kicked out of so many places it's a wonder you bother going into town. I don't know how much more of this me and Barb can take."

William managed a small chuckle. "Now you're exaggerating. It won't happen again, I promise."

Marie leaned back into her seat, disappearing into the darkness once again. "What number is this promise now? Have we hit the hundreds yet?"

As Barb leaned forward, I realized it was my turn. Barb was usually the quieter of the two. Usually. My foot went down a little harder on the gas pedal, hoping to get us home a little faster. "And you're not much better, either. If he wants to fight, you let him. That doesn't mean you have to do every damn thing he does. Use that brain of yours that you're so damn proud of."

I have a bad habit of trying to rationalize things a little too much. "But he's my friend! I didn't want to fight but he might have been...."

She disappeared into the darkness. "I don't want to talk about it."

William looked over at me and gave me his "we tried our best but what are we supposed to do?" smile. Then it was my turn to give him my "shut up and let them cool off or I'll let you walk home" look, and my attention returned to the road.

We had just turned off at country road 22 and were within fifteen minutes of getting to the Reserve. Other than our little incident, it had been a very quiet night, and we had passed only three cars in the twenty-five minute trip home. Most people didn't like to drive in the rainy weather we'd been having because it tended to freeze when it got dark, so we had the highway to ourselves. I turned the radio on.

Some soft and loving Beatles tune came flooding through the car, which badly needed it. After a while, it seemed to cut through the tension like our car was cutting through the fog.

A few minutes later, William peered out of his own little world to try some small talk. "Hey Andrew, going hunting next week?"

"Don't think so." I had been invited by my uncles but, because of some college stuff, I had to hang around the village. Everybody in the community always looked forward to hunting season—tasting the venison or moose before the car even left the driveway.

"I think I'm going with Mitch. He said he has room in his car. Can't turn down a free space now, can I?" As I said, William is more into this he-man, outdoorsy-type stuff. Me, I'd rather go to a movie. "Gee, you haven't been out hunting with us in a long time, buddy."

This was true. I've bagged my share of deer in the past, but I seemed to be more occupied with school in the last few years. And, unfortunately, hunting season and college start about the same time of year. Nowadays, I hunt books in the library.

"Bring me back a nice big steak, will you? It will just about make up for my swollen fist."

"You got it."

Out of the back seat I heard a polite if impatient "ahem" from my side of the car. That was definitely a signal to me.

"Better make that two steaks."

"Consider them in your frying pan, Andrew my buddy. You know me, I haven't come back yet without something bagged. It's that fearless hunter in me, our noble ancestors coming through my trigger finger. And if somebody else in the back seat is nice to me, I could bring back some extra steaks."

William waited expectantly, hoping to buy his way out of the trouble he was in. Marie's immediate family consisted mostly of women, many of whom married white men. So the influx of fresh deer or moose meat was very limited in their household.

As William guessed, his bait was being nibbled at. "That's cheating," came the voice from behind.

"That's love," came William's response.

Again Marie's face appeared beside William's. "Why can't I ever stay mad at you?"

"Because, as you've often told me, I'm a boy in adult's clothing and you have a maternal instinct a mile wide. It's a match made in Heaven."

"I wouldn't exactly say Heaven but it's close enough. Okay, I'll let you off the hook, again." She leaned over and kissed him on the cheek. Unfortunately, it was just below his newly swollen eye and I could see him wince. But, like the man he claims to be, he didn't utter a whimper. He was too relieved to be back in Marie's good graces. Now that left only one other matter to be resolved.

And that matter was still growling behind me in the darkness. "I suppose you want to be forgiven too?" came the voice of doom.

I answered honestly. "Not if it's gonna get me into more trouble."

She was honest too. "I don't know yet."

Sensing a warming of the cold war, William punched me in the shoulder. "It's a beginning." I turned to respond with my available arm but, was stopped by one of the voices from the back.

"Come on, you two, not in the car."

Then came the deafening screams from behind and an ugly thump at the front of the car, making us swerve uncontrollably. Something, incredibly quickly, flew up the hood and slammed into the windshield, cracking it almost totally with fine web-like fissures from side to side.

I hit the brakes and turned the wheel instinctively. The tires on the pavement screeched almost as loudly as the voices from the back, and I even heard a note or two from William as he grabbed the dashboard in front of him. Thanks to superior driving skills and a certain amount of luck, we managed to find a somewhat jarring home in the ditch.

We sat there for a moment, only the sound of our heavy breathing and heartbeats audible in the dark car. Through the faint moonlight now appearing through the fog, I looked at William, and he looked at me. I figured we both had pretty well the same expression on our faces.

"Is everyone okay. Marie? Barb? You?"

Nobody answered off the bat. I don't think they remembered they could talk.

"William, you can let go of the dashboard, now. We've stopped." I didn't recognize the sound of my voice.

William finally found his voice. "What the hell was that?! Did you see it? I think we hit something. Are you two okay? Huh?"

We both turned in our seats to check on the girls. Marie had her head in her hands, Barb was sitting on the floor.

William leaned over into the back seat and grabbed Marie's arm. "Hey Babe, you okay? Hit your head or something?"

As she took William's hand she shook her head. "No, just got a headache, that's all. I'm okay." Beside her, Barb tried to crawl out from under the seat. I tried to help but I think I just got in the way. Marie gave her a hand more successfully. "Hey, you okay Barb?"

Barb nodded at her, managed a feeble smile, then turned to me. "Andrew, what happened?"

I was so happy to see that smile, no matter how feeble it was, under the circumstances.

"I think we hit something, sweetheart, but I don't know what. You sure you're okay?"

This time her smile was stronger as she nodded.

I turned around in my seat to try to see where we were exactly, but it was virtually impossible to see out of the cracked windshield. It was like trying to look through a frosted window. William was looking out his passenger window, craning his head for a peek.

"I think I see something." He turned to me. "Well, shall we go investigate? See what trouble we're in now?"

We cautiously got out of the car, keeping the headlights on. Luckily we had skidded backend into the ditch, so the front of the car faced the road for the most part. At least we had some lighting to investigate what had hit us. Or, more correctly, what we had hit. Barb and Marie got out too, but they stayed by the car, not willing to see what remained of the thing on the road. To tell you the truth, that wasn't high on my list of preferences either.

As we slowly approached, the lump on the road took gradual shape. Even in the shadows of this deserted road, you could tell what it was. William smiled. "Well, buddy, speak of the devil. Congratulations, you got to bag your first deer of the season without leaving home. Nice sized one too."

It was a pretty expensive deer, judging by the cost of the windshield, the front bumper and hood, and God knows what else it had done to the tire alignment when we hit the ditch. I'd be lucky if this little deer didn't ratio out to at least $8.00 a pound.

Marie, rubbing her arms in the cool autumn night, yelled out to us impatiently. "Well, what is it? It's not a person, is it?"

William slapped me on the back. "No, Hawkeye here just hit tomorrow night's dinner. It's a deer."

The girls looked at each other, then hobbled up the ditch and over to where we were standing. The four of us stood there looking down at the crumpled body lying in the middle of the road. It was a good sized deer, a female, legs spread out like a sleeping dog. I like deer meat but I still could feel a bit of sadness looking at the delicate creature on the pavement in front of us. I'm sure the girls felt the same.

"Oh, how sad. How old do you think it is?"

William kneeled down to examine the head. "I'd say three years old, maybe four."

Marie asked, "So what are you going to do with it? Just leave it here?"

Still kneeling, William started rubbing his hands in anticipation. "Well, technically it's up to Andrew here, but we shouldn't let something like this go to waste. I say we take it home and eat it. Andrew?"

"Should we, Andrew?" asked Barb.

They all looked at me, and I looked at the deer. The deer was already dead, and it would be a terrible waste to let it just rot or be picked apart by local dogs and such. And maybe I could sell some of the meat to pay for the car. That was illegal but no one would tell. And there was precedent for it. Every couple of years something like this happened and we called it "deer from Heaven." Somebody on the Reserve was even talking about offering some sort of deer/car insurance.

"You're right, no sense in wasting it. Let's take it home then. Barb, see if you can get the car out of the ditch. The keys are in the ignition. William, shall we?"

Barb turned to return to the car and Marie stepped back, giving us room to grab and lift the deer. William bent to grab the front legs while I got the rear legs. We lifted together but only got the animal about a foot off the ground when William let go of the legs, letting the animal drop with a thud.

"William, quit kidding around."

At first William was silent, just staring down at the deer, then he looked up at me. There was genuine concern in his voice. "Andrew, I don't think it's dead."

Sure enough, when I looked down, two big, brown, terrified eyes were staring up at us from the formerly dead deer. Marie uttered a squeal as she clasped her hands over her mouth and stepped back. I wasn't far behind her. Even William took a surprised hop backwards.

The deer was very much alive, moving even. Evidently it had only been unconscious before, only seeming dead. It kept trying to right itself, to stand, but something was wrong. The poor thing seemed off balance, uncoordinated. It just couldn't get legs and body stabilized. It's front hooves scraped the pavement as they vainly tried to support the animal's weight.

Marie spoke the words I had been wondering: "What's wrong with it?"

The deer tried to stand again but immediately fell over, like a newborn puppy, or the newborn Bambi in that movie. It couldn't stay on its feet. But it kept trying.

William slowly circled the animal, watching it closely. "Its back's broken." William was right. The deer's hindquarters were not moving or functioning in any way. From the mid back to the tail, nothing moved of its own accord. Like dead weight. Behind us I could hear the wheels spinning in the soft damp mud as Barb vainly tried to move the car. It seemed the car was unable to move much either.

"Ooh, the poor thing," was all any of us, specifically Marie, could say as we watched the deer give up on trying to walk. Instead, still terrified, it was using its front legs to crawl away. The hooves would scratch across the pavement, straining to pull the rear end of the animal a few inches. After going a foot, the animal stopped, exhausted but still terrified. Then it tried to stand again, but with the same results. It lay there, in the middle of the road, practically bissected by the yellow line.

None of us had moved. Barb joined us, cursing to herself: "No damn good, the car's deep in the mud. Who moved the deer?" Then she saw it lift its head and look at her. "Oh my God...," was her only response.

The paralysed animal started to crawl again. Even in the bad light, from a dozen feet away, it was easy to see and hear the desperation of the deer as it tried to get away.

"William, what should we do?" I was afraid of his answer.

"I don't think it's a matter of choice. Meat aside, we've got to kill it. We can't let it suffer."

One of the girls, I don't know which, moaned a note of sadness. William noticed this. "Have either of you two got a better idea? Think we should just let it go and crawl off into the woods and die of starvation, or be attacked by dogs?"

The girls just looked at each other. They knew we had to kill the deer—we all did. It was as necessary as killing a rabid dog, but it was not a decision any one of us had expected or wanted to make. I guess it's natural to be repulsed by the need to kill, on purpose, a wounded, defenceless creature.

It was Marie who spoke first: "Yes, I guess we have to. Ooh, the poor thing."

"It would be worse if we didn't, Marie. Think about that."

It was my turn to ask a question that had been formulating in my mind since the obvious need to put the deer out of its misery had become evident. Again, I was afraid of the answer.

"Um, William, how are we going to kill it?"

He looked at me, confused for a moment, then the reality of the question sunk in.

"I don't suppose you have a rifle in the trunk of your car, Andrew?" he asked hopefully. I shook my head. I don't even own a gun. The few times I had gone hunting I had borrowed an uncle's.

"Damn." I agreed. A crippled and mangled deer crawling across the highway in front of us and no way to kill it mercifully.

"What do we do then?"

"Do you have anything? Anything at all?"

I looked through my jacket pockets and held up a pocket knife. William shook his head. "That won't do much."

Marie stepped forward a little to within a few feet of the struggling animal.

"Well, we can't let it suffer. I know this is going to sound cruel but maybe...like...we can run it over again? That should do it, shouldn't it?"

Barb joined her by the deer, shaking her head. "No can do, the car's stuck." Other than their voices, the only noise filling the night was that of hooves scratching on pavement.

William shrugged his shoulders. "Well, I'm outta ideas. Andrew?"

Unfortunately, I had an idea. I didn't want to but it was there, in the back of my mind, screaming, "it's the only logical thing to do." I hate it when my mind does things like that. I swallowed and looked at William. He could tell I had come up with something.

"I do have an idea. You won't like it. I certainly don't. But I can't come up with anything else." William looked at me expectantly. The girls turned to hear my idea too. I swallowed again.

"In the trunk. I have a tire iron."

Both girls, once it sunk in, looked like they were going to cry. They grabbed each other's hands.

William, on the other hand, looked towards the deer, his face quite grim.

"Yeah, that would do it. Can't say it will be pretty but.... No other choice, I guess." He looked at me. "Well, let's do it. Get it over with."

I got the keys from Barb, who looked on the edge of tears. I wasn't much better. I knew I wouldn't cry but there were a million other places I would rather be at that moment, including back at the bar wrestling with the bouncer. And I'm pretty sure William wasn't enjoying it either.

Silently, except for the rusty groans and creaks of the trunk, we both got the tire iron. I'd only used it three times since I had bought it with the car—all three times to fix flat tires. I felt the weight in my hand. It certainly would do the job. Strangely enough, it felt good resting in my palm. We headed back to the middle of the road, having gotten our shoes and pant legs muddy. The girls were watching us as we approached. They moved aside, back towards the car, not that I could blame them. I wished I could go with them.

By this time, the deer had made it almost to the other ditch. Another foot and it would be on the dirt shoulder. It craned its head as we came closer, and yet again we saw it futilely try to rise up and run. Instead, it resembled a grotesque marionette with broken strings.

William touched my shoulder. "Do it, man. Then let's go home. Make it quick."

This had become one of those moments we all face in life when you would gladly and willingly offer up a couple of fingers or even an eye just for a good, legitimate, reason to stop. But there was no such offer in the air. It had to be done and I had the tire iron in my hand.

I stood over the deer, looking down at those inoffensive eyes, and the weight of the iron became heavier. I tried to imagine the iron coming down on the deer's forehead, the quickest way to do it. I remembered all the deer meat I'd eaten over the years, all the deer I'd hunted. But it's different when it comes to a paralysed doe and a simple, crude tire iron. As much as I knew I had to, I just couldn't do it.

"I can't do it, William. I just can't. My arm won't go up. I keep seeing Bambi. You do it."

For the first time I thought I saw fear in William's eyes.

"Sure you can, Andrew. It has to be done."

"Then you do it." I tossed the iron to him and he caught it instinctively. But he looked at it like it was dripping with some sort of plague.

"The hell I will. You hit the deer. It was your car. You finish it."

He tossed it back to me. I tossed it back to him.

"I don't think so. You wanted to go out tonight. You got us in trouble and made us come home early. And it was you who punched my arm and caused me to hit the damn thing. You kill it. You're the fearless warrior, remember? Prove it"

I stepped back, making it perfectly clear that I had no intention of giving in. I looked at him as sternly as I could and he actually seemed to cave in. His fingers wrapped tightly around the tire iron, he approached the deer. It struggled a few inches more as William raised his arm, holding the tire iron aloft like a torch. It hovered up there before it came down. Quite slowly. Then it was dropped on the ground with a clang.

William barely whispered the words: "I can't do it either, Andrew. I tried, I really did, but like your arm wouldn't go up, my arm wouldn't go down. Christ, I've shot enough deer over the years, but I can't kill this one. I can't kill it, Andrew. I know I should, but it just looks at me with those goddamn eyes and I don't know what to do." This was the most emotional I'd ever seen him. In all the years we'd known each other, I'd never seen him crack like this. He kicked the iron towards me.

"Like I said, I can't do it. And I don't think...in fact I'm positive the girls wouldn't do it. So it's up to you, buddy. Either you take care of it, or we just leave it here and walk away. Some choice huh?"

As they say, the ball was back in my court. I could see the tire iron lying on the glistening pavement half way between me and the deer, who was on the road shoulder by now. Scarcely breathing, I bent over and picked it up.

I clenched my fist around it and approached the deer for the final time. I passed William who didn't say anything. In fact, he moved back to give me more room. Once again I stood over the exhausted deer. This time the hand holding the tire iron rose into the dark, damp air. It hovered there for a moment. I could hear the girls cry out as the damn thing came down. Quickly.

The rest of the drive home was quiet. It took about fifteen minutes for me and William to get the car out of the ditch. The girls said hardly a word, with just the occasional sob coming from the darkness. William looked out the window, quieter than usual, even moody. I didn't feel anything, or, more accurately, I didn't allow myself to feel anything. Not right now, anyway. Besides, I had to concentrate on driving with the cracked glass and the fog. That sounded like a good excuse.

We had left the deer hanging up in a tree so no animals could get at it. Somebody from the village would pick it up eventually, either for the meat or to take to the dump. We really didn't care anymore. We just wanted to get home.

William rolled down his window, letting the cold autumn air pour in through it. It felt refreshing, almost cleansing. The wind did wild, magical things with his long hair.

"Goddamn deer. Went and ruined the whole evening," was all he could say.

Someday

The snow was getting harder and harder to shovel. Twenty-six years seems old enough to get winded after the thirtieth or thirty-fifth shovelful of snow. Especially that wet, heavy type that God seems to have invented to torture people with driveways. The ironic thing is that it wasn't even my driveway. It belonged to my sometimes girlfriend, Barb. I say "sometimes" because our relationship is kinda unique: sometimes we love each other, the rest of the time we fight horrendously, sort of like a cross between a cheap motel and D-Day.

One of the things we most often disagree about is the way she has of making me do things around her house. So here I was, stooped, flinging snow and forcibly singing Christmas carols, "'tis the season to be jolly" and all that sort of stuff. But secretly, I never did put up much of a fight. Barb lived with her mother, Anne. Anne was a wonderful old woman with a perpetually full pot of tea. Barb used to have a brother, but he had died some years earlier in a car accident. The father had long since passed away of cancer, so it was just the two of them in that old house down by the lake, or so I thought.

Ever since I can remember, there had been a secret in that family. Not a terrible secret, mind you, but a painful one nevertheless. It seems that about thirty-five years ago, Anne had given birth to another child, her first. A little baby girl by the name of Mary. Her husband was in the army at the time, but nobody outside our village knew they were married. There had been rumours that the Army forced Indians to give up their Indian Status. So Frank didn't tell anybody he was Indian. He was stationed overseas and secretly sent his pay home.

This left Anne to raise her daughter alone. But it wasn't

long before the Children's Aid Society got wind of it. Back then, they had a dim view of single parents on the Reserve. In order to protect her husband, she claimed that the child's father was long gone. In those days, the government had two ways of handling things like this: send the kids off to residential schools (which they often did anyways), or, if they were younger, take them into foster homes. Little Mary was less than a year old when she was taken away, just before her first Christmas. The village rallied around Anne, but Native people could do nothing but suffer in silence back then. Time passed, her husband came home, and a few years later another child was born and then another. Both of these kids were spoiled rotten by Anne as a way of making up for her lost child, and Barb relished in it. That's why I, not Barb, was shovelling their driveway.

Anne didn't talk about Mary much. It seemed to methat it was nothing more than a distant memory for the rest of the family. But every once in a while, sometimes as Anne was cooking a big meal for all her nephews, nieces, cousins etc., or when she was at the Pow Wow, she would wonder aloud. She seemed confident that she would see Mary again. Most of her family, even Barb, tried to discourage her from this kind of talk like it was opening up old wounds. But every once in a while, Anne would talk to me about her Mary. It was sad, but I guess a part of Annie liked being sad.

"Someday she'll come home. There'll be a day when my little Mary will be standing in front of me. And I'll give her such a hug. Someday." She always said it in a wistful sort of way, but tinged with hope. In a way I felt sad for her, but in other ways I admired her confidence, her belief that she would see her daughter again after thirty-five years. Personally, I have trouble waiting for a pizza.

Unlike many cultures, the Native community respects and honours the older people of the village. Living through all those years has given them wisdom and knowledge. Anne was no different, and when it came to Mary, she simply knew. It was about a week before Christmas when the call came.

Vanessa, the receptionist at the Band office, was the one who got the call, and then phoned Anne. But it was Barb who answered.

"Barb, I just got off the phone with some woman from Toronto."

"Thank you for phoning me up and telling me that." Barb could have a sharp tongue when she wanted to.

"No, you don't understand. She was looking for some information, some old information."

"Why are you bothering me with all this? I don't care."

"Barb, listen, she wants information from about thirty-five years ago. She wanted to know if there had been any children given up for adoption way back then. She says she wants to find her family."

I couldn't hear what was going on, but by the sudden change in expression, I knew it was something heavy. Barb's eyes darted to the livingroom where her mother was watching television. She seemed to study her mother, then quickly scribbled something down on a piece of paper. Her hand was shaking.

Barb joined me at the kitchen table, forgetting her coffee by the phone. She looked funny, sort of scared, apprehensive, nervous. She told me about the call and my head immediately swivelled to Anne in the living room.

"You should tell her."

Barb shook her head. "Why? It might not be her. Why get Mom all excited?"

"Thirty-five years ago. A woman. Come on, Barb, I think you should tell her. And you know Vanessa, pretty soon the phone will be ringing off the hook. Half the village will know by dark."

I'd never seen Barb so indecisive. If it were anything less serious, I would've teased her about it. She looked at her mother again and got up. She seemed to be psyching herself up as she walked towards her. I debated whether to leave or not. This was one of those very private family moments that I really didn't want to see. In the end I stayed, thinking I could be of some help, a shoulder to lean on or something like that.

I couldn't hear them, the television was on too loud—one of Anne's favourite soap operas, something about Mike sleeping with Mitch's old girlfriend who was somehow tied up with a drug smuggling ring and the father of Mike's stepsister. All I could see was Barb kneeling in front of Anne, talking directly into her face. Even from the kitchen, I saw Anne's eyes widen, then look out the window.

Barb made me make all the necessary calls. She was too scared, and Anne was incapable of dialing the numbers. On the piece of paper that Barb gave me was a number and a strange name, not Mary's. I listened to the phone ringing all those miles away. For some reason, I was half wishing that nobody would pick up the phone, but you don't always get what you want, even at Christmas.

"Good afternoon, Bain, Williams, and Barnes. Can I help you?" Lawyers. It figures. Everybody on the outside does everything through lawyers.

"Yes, could I talk to Janice Wirth please?" I put my hand over the phone. "This must be her lawyer."

I heard the words "One moment please," and then the familiar beeping of being on hold. My eyes darted back and forth between Barb's nervous and Anne's pleading but curious eyes. Then I heard another voice on the other end.

"Janice Wirth."

"Ah yes, I believe you called the Otter Lake Reserve earlier today. I'm calling on behalf of the family you were inquiring about."

There was a slight pause. "This family had a baby girl thirty-five years ago?"

"That's correct." Her voice had that very professional tone that many of my teachers at college had. A sort of no nonsense, tell me what I want to know or I haven't got the time for you kind of voice. Yet in a way it was hesitant.

"And what was this girl's name?"

"It was Mary."

"Oh my God!" I thought that was somewhat of a strong

reaction for a lawyer. "Are you part of the family?"

"No, just a friend of the family. Um, they're very anxious to meet with Mary, her mother especially. What exactly is the procedure for this type of thing?"

"How many are there in the family? The mother's still alive, is the father? What about brothers and sisters?" She became more and more excited. I should have realized it then, but I really wasn't enjoying being in the middle of this.

"Wouldn't it be better if Mary talked with the family about all this? It's between them and her, I believe."

There was another pause. "I am Mary." Now it was my turn to pause. Anne and Barb could tell something had thrown me off. They huddled closer towards me as their eyes asked questions.

I managed to sputter out, "But you're name's Janice Wirth?"

Her voice was losing the excitement and taking on the professional tone again.

"When I was adopted, my new parents christened me Janice after a grandparent. It's only recently that I discovered my birth name was Mary."

I was taking this all in, trying to figure out a way to relate it to Barb and Anne. Again I covered the receiver and looked at Anne. "I'm talking to Mary." How I said it so matter of factly, I don't know. Anne stared at me for a moment, then the tears came. She immediately grabbed Barb and gave her as fierce a bear hug as her 100 pound body could allow her. It's been a while since I'd seen her that happy. Barb was in a daze. I asked Anne if she wanted to talk to Mary, or Janice, or whatever they decided to call her.

But Anne shook her head, she wasn't ready. She backed away from the phone like it was red hot. "I don't want to meet her over the phone. Tell her to come here, come home, as soon as possible." Again, I was left to make all the plans for the meeting. Janice was to come out to the Reserve, several hours outside the city, this weekend, just a few days before Christmas.

Anne had this calm smile on her face, but her eyes were sparkling. "This is the most wonderful Christmas present I could ever ask for." She looked up at the heavens. "Thank you Lord, my baby's coming home." She looked at me again. "I told you someday my baby would come home." Her voice had that same sense of wistfulness and hope about it, but now the sadness was gone.

The next two days were spent in feverish anticipation. Anne cleaned her house, and cleaned it again, and yet again. The old house was sparkling. Anne had been born in that house and had raised her kids there. It was over ninety years old and was constantly being renovated, but nothing could hide the slant. The house had an obvious lean to the left; Barb once called it the Communist house. Years ago the Band Office offered to build her a new house, but she declined. "I was born in this house, and I'll die in this house." But she did agree to let them install plumbing and a bathroom. "Sixty years of going to the outhouse in January is enough for any sane woman." The outhouse is still out back, almost overgrown by bushes.

All through the day, amidst the aroma of Windex and Mop N'Glo, Anne talked nonstop about Mary's visit. She had the whole weekend planned out. Anne's intention was to pack thirty-five years into two days. Everything was brought out to show her, pictures of Frank and one lone photograph of Mary as a baby. It was Anne's pride and joy.

And as the day grew closer, Barb began showing some enthusiasm about the impending visit. She even went out and chopped down a Christmas tree, and Anne said that Mary could help them put it up. "She'll be a real part of the family then."

"I'm worried about Mom." I was helping Barb untie the tree from the car. Anne was still puttering around inside, looking for non-existent dirt and dust to clean up. "What if Mary isn't what she expects?" she continued, "what if Mary doesn't like us?"

I tried to reassure Barb, but the doubts still plagued her.

"I've even gotten religious this Christmas. I've been praying that this whole thing goes right. I can handle it if Mary turns out to be a bitch or something, but Mom.... What do you think will happen?"

I shrugged. It was a big tree, hard to handle. "Don't worry about it. It's Christmas, remember, you're supposed to be jolly. You're mom's strong. And Mary spent six months trying to find you too. It's obviously very important to her. Everything will be fine. Tomorrow you two will be the best of friends, long lost sisters. It'll make a great movie-of-the-week." She laughed and shoved the tree into my ribs. We dumped it on the driveway. I'd bring it in the house tomorrow for the newly reformed family to decorate.

Tomorrow finally came. I was invited to be there for Mary's arrival. As much as I was happy for them, I really didn't want to be there. This was family business, personal business. Besides, "The Grinch Who Stole Christmas" was on television.

The atmosphere in the now pristine and spotless kitchen was tight. Fingers drummed on tables, tea was consumed in massive quantities, and, as a result, toilets were flushed, and heads were constantly swivelling towards the window overlooking the driveway.

Finally, we heard a car coming down the road. We all looked at each other, not sure how to react. Anne got up and looked out the window. She stood there for a moment, silhouetted against the winter glare. Then Barb and I joined her, scanning the white expanse of their front yard.

It was a car Janice Wirth would drive, not Mary Wabung. It was one of those foreign cars, I think a Saab. It was beautiful and that seemed to clash with the dirt driveway. The car crept forward almost as if it were afraid of the little house.

There's a certain knack to driving in the country, of learning how to manoeuvre on slippery dirt roads, and this woman just didn't have that knack. Twenty feet from the house, her Saab lost traction as she tried to drive around the Christmas tree. Her car plowed into the snowbank. Evidently, all my snow shovelling had done little good. For a few moments there was no movement from the car and we couldn't see in. It just sat there for what seemed an eternity. Then the door opened and she got out.

At first she appeared to be a white blur, then we realized it was the fur coat she was wearing. It seemed to swell and ebb in the wind coming off the lake, like it was still alive. Evidently Mary/Janice had done very well for herself. She stood at the front of the house, gazing at it. There was no discernable expression on her face, except curiosity. She was drinking everything in, putting pieces back into the puzzle. Anne was the first to move. She ran to the door and flung it open. Mary's eyes met Anne's. No words were spoken, they just looked at each other. It finally dawned on me that it was minus fifteen degrees and Anne was standing out there on the steps with just a blouse on. I nudged Barb, who was also staring.

"Mom, invite her in." Barb had to say it a second time before Anne responded, somewhat embarrassed.

"I'm sorry. Mary, please come in. You must be cold."

At first Mary didn't move, then she slowly made her way to the steps. Her shoes weren't made for walking on hard-packed snow. She almost slipped twice before she made it to the relative safety of the steps. She slowly climbed them, getting closer and closer to Anne. It was almost like slow motion. Finally, they were barely inches apart.

Even from inside the house I could see familiar things in Mary's unfamiliar face, like Anne's eyes, and the little bump on Barb's nose. She wore more make-up than Barb, but their hair had the same texture.

"Baby, my baby!" Anne threw her arms around her child and hugged her tightly. Mary was startled and tried to return the hug but didn't know how to. She glanced over our way and spotted Barb. It was their time to stare at each other. Again, it was Anne who broke the silence.

"Mary, this is your sister Barbara."

"My sister...?!"

Uncharacteristically, Barb just nodded and once again I

wondered what the hell I was doing there. Finally she looked at me.

"Just a friend," I answered quickly, "the guy on the phone."

Anne grabbed her arm with one hand as she wiped away some tears with her other hand. She directed Mary over to the kitchen table. "Welcome home. What a wonderful Christmas." It was time for the umpteenth cup of tea, then the talking started. Of course at first it was kind of hesitant and slow. Neither Barb nor Mary seemed willing to open up and talk freely yet. It was too new a situation. It was something they had all anticipated since birth but never really expected. Anne was the only one oblivious to it. She was talking a mile a minute. She persuaded Mary, who had trouble answering to that name, to tell us of her search.

"It's a long story, but all stories have a beginning, I guess. I always knew I was an Indian, but to me it was like being five foot four. It's just an interesting fact, nothing more. Then Meech Lake happened with Elijah Harper, then Oka. Back at the office, all my colleagues would ask me my opinion—the Native opinion on the situation. The only opinion I could give came from Willowdale. The more questions I got asked, the more questions I had. It reached a saturation point where I resolved to find out about my beginnings.

"It wasn't easy. A lot of doors were slammed in my face, but I carried on. I went to the city I was adopted in, found the court I was processed in and requested my adoption papers. Once I had those, I contacted the Department of Indian Affairs, presented them with the information I had, and they told me what Reserve I was from. Then I called here. Then you called me. Now I'm here."

There was an awkward silence. Then Barb asked about her childhood and Mary opened up. She had grown up in a fairly prosperous home. Unlike many Native adopted children, she had no horror stories to tell. Both sides felt more comfortable. And Anne was fairly glowing. They talked for hours, consuming at least four pots of tea. I could barely get a word in edgewise. I just sat there, nodding my head. But you can only nod your head for so long. Desperate to say something, I complimented her on her car.

"My car! How am I gonna get it out of that snow bank? Is there a towing service nearby?" Bingo, I couldn't have asked for a better excuse to get out of there. "You don't need a tow truck for that. I'll take care of it." I got up. The third wheel was rolling out of there. I got my jacket and boots on and tried to wave good bye, but I didn't exist for them at that moment. So I stepped out on the porch, grabbed the shovel and checked out how far into the snowbank the car had gone. It wasn't that bad. I'd have it out in half an hour.

Even though I was glad at the chance to leave them alone, I was less than pleased about the prospect of shovelling more snow. But I gritted my teeth and went at it. I could see them moving about the kitchen, getting more tea, going to the bathroom. The sun was setting over the frozen lake and it was cold, but I felt warm. It was Christmas—Anne had her daughter back, Barb would be happy for a while. All was right with the world. I looked over at the Christmas tree lying at the side of the road and made a mental note to take it in before I left, and let them do the family thing with it.

I had just about finished when the door opened and Mary emerged. She had that enormous white fur coat on and came floating down the steps. Trying not to fall, she walked over towards her car.

"Oh thank you. I hoped you'd be finished by now. Am I supposed to tip you or anything like that?" Not knowing if she was kidding, I shook my head.

"Okay, well thank you again. Bye."

"You're leaving? Already? You just got here a couple of hours ago! They had all sorts of things planned for you."

"I know, and I hated to disappoint them, but I do have other appointments to keep. I hope they won't be too distraught."

I plunged my shovel into the snow and leaned against the Saab. I was trying to figure her out. "You gave them a special Christmas. I think they wanted to share that with you."

"Well, sometimes you can't always get what you want."
I remembered thinking that on the phone.

"Mary...."

"Please, call me Janice."

"Janice, why did you come out here?"

"Curiosity. I had to know. I had to see. So now I know and
I've seen what I wanted to see."

I followed her eyes as they wandered over thc house. They
went from the half-hidden outhouse out back to the dirt
driveway to the leaning wooden house. I decided to push the
issue. "When do you think you'll be back?"

Her eyes finally ended up at the two uneven figures
standing quietly in the window. "Oh, someday, I suppose."
There was that same tone of wistfulness and sadness I
recognized, but no hope. She opened her car door and got
in. She looked at me, and I looked at her.

"Merry Christmas" was all she said.

With obvious care, she backed her car up and drove away.
My last image of Janice was her personalized license plate.
"WIRTH" disappearing in the distance.

I turned around to face the house and noticed the
two images in the window had disappeared. I admit it, I was
half tempted to call it a day, to just go home and drink
as much egg nog as I possibly could. There are many things
in this world that make me uncomfortable. What had
happened in that house was one of them. I threw the shovel
in the snowbank and looked longingly across the frozen bay
to my house.

Instead, I bent and picked up that big old spruce
Christmas tree. Gripping it tightly, I knew it would be a bitch
getting it up those slippery steps.

Heat Lightning

Off in the distance, across the calm blue lake, I could see the heat lightning flash, making the large, fluffy clouds glow and shimmer like a scene from a Steven Spielberg movie. My friend Jamie's house stood on the eastern end of the lake, so from the shore you could always see the dark and heavy storms rolling in over the dark blue water.

Luckily this kind of lightning had nothing to do with the violent thunderstorms you usually see during the summer— these were just nature's way of letting off electrical stress. You couldn't even hear the thunder. You could just see the lighting illuminate the clouds from the interior like a flashlight under a blanket. And there was never any rain, just the promise of it.

Had it been a real storm coming, no doubt Jamie would have had us working double time. He can be kind of serious when the mood strikes him. As it was, we were quite busy sharing a beer as we watched nature's fireworks, sitting atop the pile of lumber lying between the house and the lake. The renovations to his mother's house could wait a few minutes more. Rome wasn't built in a day and we weren't in any mood to defy the cliché.

Jamie was half Ojibway, half Mohawk. Guess that makes him an Oji-hawk, I suppose. An odd mixture for the likes of this community. With this being a strictly Ojibway village and us being hereditary enemies with the Mohawks not more than just a few centuries ago, this might have caused some problems, if not just a whole lot of teasing. But this is Otter Lake and being an Oji-hawk was the least of Jamie's problems.

I drained my beer. "How long will this take? The whole thing I mean? Some of us start college next week, you know."

Jamie shrugged, his brown eyes never leaving the

lightning. He had that look of a great weight behind his eyes that he sometimes gets when things aren't going well. "It will take as long as it takes. Hopefully not longer than Friday. Plenty of time for you to go off and chase white girls. One of these days you might actually catch one and get lucky."

"You forget. With Mohawks, it's luck. With Ojibways it's skill."

Jamie smiled. I was the only one who teased him about his unusual bloodline and just that alone. I think he liked and appreciated me for it. Unlike a lot of the locals, I never commented on his home life or his mother, or made the rude remarks that got him into so many fights as a kid, and also occasionally as an adult. I think that's probably why he asked me to help renovate his mother's house. That and the fact he needed my pickup for all the lumber.

He stood and stretched, the rip in his plaid shirt showing his untanned side. I placed the empty beer in the twelve pack and joined him in an equally luxurious stretch.

"Well then Sailor...." Jamie's called me that ever since he saw a twenty-year-old photograph of me wearing an idiotic sailor's hat my mother had found in a rummage sale and forced me to wear. As I said, teasing can be quite unmerciful on Reserves. "Let's get back to work. There's a wall over there with our names on it."

He was referring to his mother's bedroom wall which looked out over the lake. Practically the whole side of the room had been removed to put in a large picture window with a sliding glass door. Next on the list was to put a deck on the outside of that door, but I had my fingers and other parts of my body crossed in hope that that was going to wait until next year. Jamie loved his mother, but not that much.

We picked up pretty well where we left off fifteen minutes earlier, struggling to fit the new frame for the doorway into place. The picture window was already fixed in position, just waiting for the glass door to complete the framing. But the door was being difficult. It was an old house and it had settled in some pretty peculiar ways, as old houses often do, and I got the feeling it didn't like the cosmetic surgery we were performing.

"Come on Sailor, force it!" was the only encouragement I got from Jamie. Being equally adept with a grunt I answered, "I am, but it won't go. Like you and school."

He smiled again, this time through the sweat. He didn't have many friends on the Reserve, especially since he had moved to Peterborough several years ago to get away from this house. At least there, the less people knew, the better. And often, they didn't care.

He shifted his position to the inside of the house, trying to use his weight to pull the door-frame into place. He tugged at it a few times, his back hitting a large oak chest of drawers. All the glass paraphernalia on its top clinked together like bottles in a liquor cabinet.

Giving me a frustrated look, Jamie leaned against the dresser and yelled through the open door to the rest of the house.

"Hey Mom, we gotta move this dresser or we'll knock something over. Is that okay?"

There was a rustling from the kitchen before Jamie's mother, Patricia, or Patty as we called her appeared. She looked a lot like Jamie but obviously older and a bit heavier. She didn't have Jamie's hard look, but then again he didn't have her dreamy quality either. A pity, since both could have no doubt used a bit of each other's attributes. So as it stood, basic appearances and blood were about the only thing those two seemed to have in common.

She smiled her Patricia smile when she saw me. "Oh hi Andrew, don't let him work you too hard. His father does that all the time to his own friends." Despite the heat of the day, I felt a chill go down my spine when she said things like that. She turned to Jamie. "You can move it, but be careful. Kathryn will take a fit if anything happens to her dresser." Her mind definitely stated, she turned and called out to the kitchen, "Kathryn, hurry up. We'll be late."

If I could read minds, I would probably have felt Jamie

wondering how long an oak dresser could float in the middle of the lake. Maybe Kathryn with it. But it was a question that would remain unanswered as Kathryn appeared in the doorway, and with this, an almost tangible change in the atmosphere of the room. And not a pleasant one, either.

Kathryn was a smart-looking white lady in her forties, a close friend of Patricia's. A more politically correct and accurate term might be partner, or bus'gim, an Ojibway term meaning girlfriend/boyfriend, and, unfortunately an even more realistic term would be Jamie's sworn enemy. Patricia and Kathryn lived together in that little house on the shore of that big lake, and that was the reason Jamie lived in town.

Jamie's Mohawk blood came from his father, Galen, who many years ago had lived and loved in this small house with Patricia. According to my mother, theirs was a passionate relationship, and they acted like newlyweds for over four years. But Galen had other passions that were equally important to him.

Two years after Jamie was born, Galen joined the American army, following a long family tradition, to go off and fight in Vietnam. I was surprised to learn that quite a number of Native people, even in Canada, had joined the American armed forces during that violent time, and Galen evidently felt the call too. I guess the Canadian Army just didn't have the mighty warrior ring to it that the Marines did.

After your standard tearful goodbye to his wife and young son, the kind you only see in Oliver Stone movies, Galen went overseas in '71. He was five months short of ending his tour of duty when the telegram came. On some sort of recon mission, Galen and his platoon came under heavy enemy fire. Only a handful made it back to camp. Galen wasn't one of them. The strange thing was that nobody actually saw him being shot, caught or anything. He had just disappeared into the jungle. His body was never found, so, as was the procedure, he was listed as missing in action.

Once, in an uncharacteristically pensive moment, Jamie had confessed to me the guilt he felt because he doesn't remember his father. There wasn't a tangible memory to grieve with sorrow, or remember with happiness. Nothing. He had just turned three when his mother went into mourning and never came out. All he can recollect of that dark time was the non-stop crying that went on for months and spending a lot of time in his room, alone. He does, however, remember suddenly appearing at his maternal grandparents' house for several months during what later turned out to be Patricia's breakdown.

Then, one sunny summer day, Jamie does recall his mother appearing in his grandmother's living room. He remembers this strange woman who looked somewhat familiar picking him up. Then, after a short car ride, he found himself in a new place that again, looked slightly familiar.

Apparently Patricia had been released from the hospital and was supposedly fit to face the world. But as most of the Reserve wondered, how fit is fit?

Patricia had seemed okay, throwing herself into the raising of her son. She'd gotten her smile back and her laugh, and gave off the air that nothing had changed. That was the first hint that something was a little off. She kept referring to Jamie as "Galen's legacy" and "how she had to look after him until Galen was found, or made his way out of the jungle, or was released, or whatever."

Since he was only MIA, he was surely alive somewhere, and she settled in to wait. Someday he would come home. However long that took.

That was over twenty years ago and her talk is still peppered with statements and certainties about Galen; Galen this and Galen that, always in the present tense like he was catching the bus home at the end of the week with his arms full of Chinese food or something. Most of us who are close to the family have gotten used to it, but if you take the time to actually think about it like I do, it'll give you the willies for sure.

For a number of years after Galen disappeared, a few of her friends and family tried to get Patricia dating again, maybe get her mind back into the real world and help her get

103

on with life. But they had about as much success as the Americans did in finding Galen.

"I can't go out with anybody!" she'd laugh, shaking her head in amazement. "I'm married, remember?" Then she'd thrust up her ring finger to remind everybody with the physical evidence. My aunt once told me she was always tempted to quote the line from the wedding vows that went "till death do you part" to Patricia, but then thought she might jinx Galen's return. Deep down inside, most of the village hoped they were wrong and Patricia was right. So, as it was, Patricia was bound and determined not to have anything to do romantically with members of the opposite sex.

"It wouldn't be right. Just imagine what Galen would say when he gets back."

Instead, still feeling the need for non-family companionship, she joined some women's organization in Peterborough after seeing something on 60 minutes about MIA wives banding together. But seeing how MIA wives were about as numerous in Peterborough as Vietnamese, she had to make do with various other women's groups.

That's where she met Kathryn, who ran one of the groups.

By this time Jamie was older. He was about ten or so when he first met Kathryn. Patricia had invited her to the Reserve for dinner and Jamie remembers them staying up all night talking. Patricia was rolling out all the Galen stories she knew and Kathryn politely listened to them all.

About six months later, Kathryn moved in, in every sense of the word. Nobody is really quite sure how it all happened, and with Otter Lake being as homophobic as any small town community, not too many people really went out of their way to find out all the dirty details. They were more than content to gossip around what little information they had. Needless to say, friends and family were shocked and scandalized, and again questioned Patricia's state of mind.

But I don't think it was insanity at work. More like loneliness. Existing in an environment of your own creation can be a solitary reality. Kathryn must have been attracted to

Patricia's...sweetness, is the only word I can come up with. Living in her own world of hope and unshakable belief had left a residual effect of some sort on most people. She is the sweetest, nicest, most giving person I have come across in my travels. Had she been twenty years younger, not Jamie's mother, and in the right state of mind, I might have been tempted myself.

As for what brought Patricia to Kathryn in particular, who can say? Perhaps she needed Kathryn's strength and leadership to lean on. Or it could be as simple as companionship? Seven years of being by yourself, with no close fellowship, either emotional or physical, is hard on anyone. And maybe this way she felt she wouldn't be cheating on Galen. Whatever the reason, they were still together all these years later.

And that's where Jamie's problems really began. Reserve life for anybody out of the ordinary is difficult enough. But for kids with...different...mothers, it can be hell. Jamie's middle name is Richard, which in turn is usually changed to Dick, but in Jamie's case, he was called Dyke.

Now this can make a kid go two ways: he can shrink into himself and live the life of a put upon wimp, or he can get tough and take on the world. The second is exactly what Jamie did. Repeatedly. Sometimes violently.

I've known Jamie all the thirteen years he's been fighting people with enough poor judgement to tease him openly, defending his mother's honour, and quietly hating Kathryn.

"She's using her. She preys on Mom." He could never bring himself to say Kathryn's name but he always had words to say about how Kathryn was some sort of Butch manipulating his dysfunctional mother.

At age sixteen he left home, moved in again with his grandparents for a couple years, then got his own place in town.

Regardless of his feelings towards Kathryn, Jamie would still come home and do things for his mother, but he would always try and arrange it for when Kathryn wasn't around.

And to her credit, Kathryn went out of her way to arrange these encounters, especially around Galen's birthday and the unmentioned D Day (Disappearance Day).

But not today. That's why we were fighting with a support beam in a large hole in the bedroom wall.

Kathryn's salt-and-pepper short hair was still damp as she put her coat on with one hand and tried to dry it with another. She too smiled when she saw me. I was one of the few locals who came to visit.

"Hey Andrew, still looking as cute as ever. You still a heart breaker?"

I should never have answered the phone last Sunday from the desperate but persuasive Jamie. He's a better carpenter than I am but, unfortunately, I was the one who owned the truck to pick up the lumber. Being mobile can have its disadvantages.

"I'm a little old to be cute," I responded.

"With a face like that, you're never too old, eh Patty?" Patricia nodded with a smile. Kathryn gently patted my face in an almost motherly fashion. Jamie's eyes never left Kathryn, who had, over the years, learned to ignore his scathing glare. He shoved the large dresser to the side with a violent thrust of his hip. The dresser and floor shrieked in protest. The little bottles of perfumes sitting atop it tinkled and jingled with the force of the movement.

"Jamie! I said be gentle with it. Your father would be ashamed!" I could never figure out if Patricia was oblivious to the less than sublime relationship of the two people closest to her or whether she chose to merely ignore it. In all the time I've know them, she has never acknowledged the cold war that raged within the confines of that house.

"Sorry mom," was all Jamie would say to her. "Come on, Sailor, give me a hand. We wouldn't want to damage this fine work of art." Embarrassed, I looked at Kathryn. She shrugged back, the retaliation of somebody used to a thousand small insults, and who couldn't be bothered.

Patricia was doing up her coat as she passed us. "Now you

boys have fun. We'll go into town so we'll be out of your way. Should be back by supper time. And we'll expect you to stay for dinner after all that hard work, Andrew. Won't we Kathryn?"

Kathryn put her towel on top of the dresser and did her own coat up. "Wouldn't have it any other way. It's always interesting to have a man in the house. There are so few good ones around."

Without looking at Jamie, I could tell that comment had struck a bull's eye. The war got colder, and so did I.

Patricia stepped out through the hole in the wall and waited for Kathryn to join her. "Tell you what, I'll make spaghetti tonight. It's Galen's favourite and I already have some sauce in the freezer. Is that okay with you boys?"

I nodded and so did Jamie. "That will be okay, Mom. See you later."

"Bye. Come along, Kathryn. You drive, okay?"

"I'd love to. And try not to work too hard, boys. Men sweat so when they try to prove too much." This was why I hated to be in the same room with the both of them at the same time. Separately, they were each fine and nothing but polite and natural to me. But put them together and the worst sides of each came out. I have an aversion to most types of wars, especially psychological ones.

Kathryn walked by Jamie with a curt "bye" and, with a genuine smile, touched my arm in a warm manner, then she was out the hole in the wall with Patricia.

Jamie was silent for a moment, then took a deep breath. "I wish she'd leave. I wish Mom would just kick her out and everything would be like it used to be." I'd heard this all before a thousand times. And a thousand times I'd tried to find different ways of changing the subject, but with little success.

"I don't think that's going to happen. And I don't think things can ever be the same until they find your father. Come on, give me a hand with the dresser."

On the wall over by the door was a picture of Galen, in his

military dress. Jamie was staring at it. In retrospect, they looked a lot alike, except Jamie was a bit heavier. Probably the Ojibway influence.

"Give me a break, my dad's dead. Everybody knows it except Mom. I've tried to tell her that a couple of times but I just can't bring myself to do it. Mom's so sure of him coming home. I don't know what to do."

He looked over at another picture on Patricia's dresser. This one was a wedding picture of Galen and Patricia and the middle right side of the frame looked unusually tarnished, as if it had been picked up a lot.

"And that woman doesn't make it any better."

I quickly grabbed the side of Kathryn's dresser and lifted my end up. "Hey you, enough talking. I have school in a couple of days. Work time."

Nodding in agreement, Jamie put the picture back down on Patricia's dresser and leaned over to grab the other end. We groaned together and lifted the heavy piece of furniture a few feet until Jamie stumbled over his own footing, smashing his shoulder against Patricia's maple dresser. I saw the marriage photograph slip from the top and, hearing me yell, Jamie made a lunge for it. Kathryn's dresser made a crash landing.

Two things happened almost immediately. Jamie caught the picture before it hit the ground, and because the dresser was left in my hands alone, it tilted, almost falling over. Half the drawers came flying out across the room. I managed to steady the thing to prevent it from falling over completely, but a definite mess had been made. The bedroom now resembled a war zone.

Jamie looked at the four drawers and their scattered contents, then at me.

"Oops," was the quintessential Jamie comment.

I quickly kneeled down and started to gather up some of the stuff; clothes, travel pamphlets, a sewing kit, and some letters. Not knowing what to do, I started randomly putting the various articles back into the drawers. I noticed Jamie wasn't helping me. He was still holding his parents' wedding picture.

"Hey, aren't you gonna help?"

"Let her clean it up. Her stuff. Wasn't our fault. It was an accident."

"Don't give Kathryn ammunition to use against you. Leave it like this and she'll think you went through her stuff." Evidently I had struck a logic cord in his head and he replaced the picture and started gathering Kathryn's clothes together.

It would be obvious to her that things in her drawers had been rearranged a bit, but we could have blamed it on moving the dresser back and forth. She's not a dumb woman, but sometimes people will believe anything, especially during house renovations.

I left Jamie to pick up the rest as I replaced the restocked drawers in what I hoped was the proper order. "Finished with the others yet?"

Turning, I saw that Jamie had a telegram in his hands. From where I stood, it looked official. But the expression on his face did not bode well. His eyes looked as strained as the hand holding the telegram. He didn't even look like he was breathing. Slowly, he started to open the letter.

"Wait a minute Jamie, that's illegal or something...?"

My warning received no reaction. He either didn't hear me, or he didn't care. Slowly he drew the telegram out of the envelope, pinching the tip of it, then let the envelope fall to the ground where I picked it up, curious.

You could tell by the insignia that it was from the United States Government. I'd recognize that self-righteous eagle anywhere. It was from the Department of Defense. It looked old.

Feeling like a cat with a canary in his mouth, I couldn't help but look around nervously. I wasn't actually doing anything wrong, but I believe I feared the guilty by association.

Jamie opened his mouth but didn't say anything. He

looked like he had no breath with which to speak. Then his hoarse and distant voice came: "August twenty-first, 1985...nine years ago...the remains of Private Galen hill were recovered...buried with full military honours... condolences...special thank you to Kathryn Sargent for arranging burial services since Patricia Hill could not be found."

The words on that telegram and the look in Jamie's eyes made the pit of my stomach dry up. The silence made it worse. Ranting and raving I could have handled—it would have been an outlet—but not the silence. His breathing was the only thing that made me conscious of time passing.

Then one deep breath, and a whisper.

"She knew. All this time she knew. And she didn't tell us! She buried my father without telling us!" His formerly cold and distant voice was now anything but. Noisily, the guilty letter was unconsciously being crumpled in his hand.

Slowly the intense look of anger dissolved into genuine sadness. "It's over. My dad is real again. He's back over here. I've got to tell Mom." Out of nowhere, his face took on the appeal of a puppy with a large soup bone in sight. I figured this particular soup bone might be named Kathryn.

This look of eagerness in his face had me worried. We were not the best of friends, him being just a little too intense for my tastes, but I knew him well enough to be concerned about his anxious and eager looks. I'd seen this look as the cause of too many fights and too much trouble.

"I guess you should. Why do you think Kathryn would have done all this? It doesn't make sense." That was the truth. I had always thought Kathryn was pretty cool as things went, but now I wasn't so sure. There was a lot here that wasn't being explained.

Jamie threw the crumpled letter against a wall. The anger was coming back. "Of course it does. I told you all along she was a bitch. Maybe now Mom will see the real her."

I chose my next words very carefully. "Jamie, just be sure you want to tell this news about your father to your mother to let her mind rest, not to get revenge on Kathryn."

He looked at me. Those brown eyes could have driven a few of the two-inch nails we'd been using through a hardwood floor. Perhaps because of this I grabbed my hammer. "Sorry, just thinking aloud. Well, let's go get that door frame, huh?"

His stare never wavered. "Whose side are you on? This is my mother we're talking about. And my father. I'm going to tell my mother about this because I care about her. That's why. She deserves to know, don't you think?"

"Hey, I'd really rather not get involved in this. You're the son, not me. I'm just hired labour."

Muttering to himself, he went out the hole in the wall and I soon could hear him struggling with some lumber. I leaned against Kathryn's dresser wondering what I'd gotten myself into. Occasionally I could hear splashes of mumbled sentences floating in from the lawn. "You have no idea. You can't. She's my mother, not yours. I know what's best for her...."

Other than the sporadic grumbling, for the rest of the afternoon we worked in silence. Or rather, I worked in silence. I don't think Jamie was really there, other than in body. It took him three times as long to do things as it did me, making me acutely aware that my plan to finish the bracing then run away and hide before the women got home was fast disappearing.

Even more discerning was Jamie's lack of interest in the quality of work he was doing. It was obvious that some of the bracing would have to be done over again, but this was not the time to inform him of this. Jamie was in his own little world and I don't think I was welcome there.

It was late in the afternoon, that golden time just as the sun is beginning to set behind the still-active clouds of heat lightning on the horizon, adding a sense of other worldliness to the summer sky. It was into this picturesque scene that the ladies arrived, arms laden with packages and groceries. This was the moment I had been fearing all afternoon.

Jamie straightened up from planing a two-by-four, and

stood tall. I mentally wondered whether, should the situation arise, I could take Jamie in a fight. Or in the prevension of one. We were about the same height, but he was a little heavier, most of it muscle – he loved to work with his hands and back more than I did. He also had done more fighting than I had. The odds were in his favour. Nothing was going right that afternoon.

As they approached, they waved, oblivious to the atmosphere. I managed a weak half-circle of my right hand and noticed, out of the corner of my eye, Jamie nodding his head almost imperceptibly in acknowledgement. Patricia yelled from the front door: "Dinner in about half an hour, boys. I hope you're hungry." Kathryn put her arm around Patricia as they entered the house. They laughed about something as the door closed behind them.

I waited nervously for some reaction, but, surprisingly, nothing happened. Clichés rushed through my mind: it's always quietest before the storm, the Natives are restless, the eye of the hurricane....

Again we went back to work until, without looking at me as he finished planing that board, Jamie spoke.

"Okay, you're the genius, what do you think I should do?"

I hunted for nails, or at least I pretended to. "Whatever you want to do."

He threw down his plane. "You're a lot of help. Not more than two hours ago you were chewing me out for wanting to do what I think is the right thing to do."

"Then do it. We both know that whatever I tell you to do, you're gonna do what you want anyway. That's the way you are. Why do you think I'm the only one here helping you with your stupid house? Nobody else would come. You give them too much of a hard time. It's your way or no way. Does any of this sound familiar?" There, I had said it. I waited for the effect.

It was one of silence. At first. "My life is my life, Sailor. I do what I want cause it gets me through. That's not an explanation, or an excuse, just the way it is. My life is a lot different from yours, way different, and I have to make do.

When you have to live with growing up in this house, talk to me then. Then you'll know why I do what I do. Speaking of which, I can also finish the house myself. Thanks for everything, Sailor." I was being dismissed. He turned and went inside the house, slapping the plastic door aside.

My pickup was waiting for me, and I had the door opened before I heard Patricia's voice calling from the kitchen window.

"Don't you dare leave this property. The spaghetti's almost cooked and we have far too much for us to eat alone."

I had been invited to dinner and Patricia was determined to make sure I was going to eat. But I was determined not to give up without a fight. Like the dark thunderclouds hanging over that little house, I knew what waited at the end of the dinner.

"I really got to get home. I sort of promised my mother...."

"Kathryn is setting the plates. You get in here right this minute." With that she slid the window closed. I was trapped. I could still get in the truck and drive away, but I couldn't do it with a clear conscience. Like a virus, Patricia has a way of worming her way into your subconscious. The door to the truck closed behind me.

The walk to the kitchen door was the longest of my life. I had never noticed how serene the house looked, with the lake as a backdrop. I could see bodies moving around in the darkness of the kitchen window. I wondered what they served at the Last Supper.

Though I'd been working all day, I had no appetite. My brain feverishly tried to come up with a logical way of getting out of dinner without insulting Kathryn and Patricia, but I had lost my only chance.

Jamie was already sitting at the table when I entered. I took the seat nearest the door, right beside him. Patricia was in mid scolding.

"Why must you always fight with everybody? You should be like your father more, everybody likes him. He has friends everywhere. And Andrew is always welcome in this house."

The room reeked of garlic and oregano. Jamie had the salt shaker clutched firmly in the palm of his hand. He was squeezing it. "You just remember that, young man. So, how're the noodles doing, Kathryn?" Without waiting for an answer, Patricia grabbed a noodle with a fork and slid it into her mouth as Kathryn finished making the garlic bread. I remembered that Kathryn was part Italian. I couldn't help thinking that there was nothing quite like a traditional Italian/Indian spaghetti dinner.

"Finished with that door yet? A cold draft comes through that thing at night, you know." That was from Kathryn.

His voice oddly calm, Jamie answered, his eyes firmly on Kathryn. "Things will be fixed up soon. Things will be just the way they used to be. Wouldn't want something like that to be bothering you for a long time. That would be wrong, eh Kathryn?"

It was the first time I'd ever heard him use her name, let alone in her presence. Kathryn's reaction was immediate, a quick look of surprise and puzzlement. You could tell she saw something unusual in the way he looked at her. Jamie had scored round one in a battle Kathryn didn't yet know was happening.

Patricia was rinsing the noodles under the tap, oblivious to what was happening behind her. "Good. I'm not your father. He loves sleeping out in the open but all the insects get to me, even with that tarp you put up."

"Yeah, Dad was kind of tough, eh Mom? Think he's still alive?"

Across the kitchen, Kathryn had turned away from Jamie and was popping the bread in the oven. When she heard this she froze over the stove. I closed my eyes, wincing. Whatever people may have thought of Patricia's living arrangement with Kathryn, there was an unspoken agreement everywhere in the Reserve not to burst her bubble about Galen being alive. You can fool around with a living person but hands off the dead ones.

The strainer of spaghetti was quietly lowered into the sink.

Kathryn and I glanced at each other briefly, wondering what Patricia's reaction would be. She hadn't moved from the sink. Her voice was remarkably controlled, quiet even, and very firm.

"Your father is too alive. They never found his body, and I know him well enough to know that men like him don't die easily. He is alive somewhere and don't you forget it!"

Jamie cleared his throat ominously. "But how can you be so sure Mom? It's been almost twenty years and...."

"I just know!" she screamed. "I made him promise me he'd come back. He promised!" Kathryn fell back against the stove, a look on her face so intense I wouldn't have thought it possible, and I closed my eyes again.

"Jamie..." I said, trying unsuccessfully to diffuse the situation.

In a whisper Jamie again asked, "Do you, Mom?"

"Jamie...." This time it was Kathryn's turn to intervene.

With a cry, Patricia reached in the sink and threw the strainer full of spaghetti across the room. Tendrils of white pasta sailed through the air, pelting Jamie. Even I felt a whip of it, still burning hot, going down the neck of my jacket.

"Don't you dare ever say anything like that! Ever again!" Patricia flew at Jamie, her arms working like a flailing machine gone crazy. She hit at him repeatedly, making the spaghetti fly again until Kathryn and I pulled her off. Fighting her way out of our arms, she ran from the kitchen and disappeared down the hallway that led to the bedroom. The house shook with the slamming of a door.

Kathryn's eyes turned in their sockets to look at us. Jamie, I, and the kitchen were a mess.

Kathryn trembled as she spoke. "What the hell is wrong with you?! Do you know what you just did?"

Without speaking, Jamie removed a piece of paper from his coat pocket. He must have recovered it from the floor when I was on my way to the truck. He smoothed it out and held it up for Kathryn to see.

Kathryn glanced quickly at the telegram. Then, almost

instantly, the emotions playing across her face fell away as others rushed in to take their place. The fierce anger that had been burning had now been replaced by wide-eyed fear as the reality of the telegram registered.

I saw a small smile, however cold, appear on Jamie's face—one of ultimate victory.

I could see a lump moving down Kathryn's throat as she swallowed. "Where'd you get that? You went rummaging through my things, didn't you?"

Jamie shook his head, ever so slowly, every movement exaggerated in his control of the situation. "No. Didn't have to. It appeared before me as God wanted it to."

You could almost see the wheels turning in Kathryn's head as explanations and excuses came and went through her mind. And Jamie sat there, quietly, waiting for them. Unfortunately, so was I.

"I can explain..." she started.

"I'm waiting" was Jamie's only response.

Kathryn paced the kitchen as Jamie watched her and I watched him. She stopped in front of the big window overlooking the driveway.

"I know you've always hated me."

His voice barked. "The telegram! Why did you hide it? Why didn't you tell me or my mother. You buried my father without telling us."

"I did it for your mother!"

"I knew you'd say something like that. Don't try and con me with all this heart-gushing over Mom. If you cared for her one little bit, if her life meant anything to you, you would have told her. You of all people know how hung up on Dad she is. This might have freed her."

Kathryn was silent for a moment, the words sinking in. "From him, or from me?"

Jamie stood up and rounded the table. "You know very well what I mean. This was just to make sure she wouldn't leave you. If she knew Dad was dead, really dead, she could go back to living a normal life."

"And just what the hell do you consider a normal life?"

"Do I have to spell it out?"

"Please."

Their eyes locked as I sat silently in my little chair at the side of the table. The storm was building.

"The truth is you didn't want Mom to get on with her life so you hid this telegram and buried him yourself to keep her with you. Didn't you? Admit it!" Instead of anger, there was amazement, almost surprise on Kathryn's face.

"After all this time, you still think I'm just playing head games with your mother? That's the only reason I'm here?"

Jamie turned away, the spaghetti falling from his shoulders. "Oh, yeah, sorry, you're a great saint who should be congratulated for making my mother a social outcast."

"Jamie, you know your mother, you should know how this would affect her. She so believes in Galen's return that nothing else has any meaning for her. Take that away...take away her faith, her reason for going on, and you might as well kill her."

"You're grasping at straws, Kathryn. This might make her stronger."

"No, it won't. If Galen dies, she dies. Think about it, Jamie. She's not very strong, never was. He's all she's ever talked about since the day I met her. He is alive to her, just like you and I am. I've know for thirteen years that if he walked in that door right now, right this minute, I wouldn't be a flicker of memory in your mother's eyes. I'd be a distant second to him. But I've accepted that and life goes on."

Kathryn leaned wearily against the sink, the strength going out of her voice. "Believe it or not, Jamie, I think I know your father as well as you do, probably better in fact. You only knew him for two years when you were a baby. I've had thirteen years of stories and legends to know him. It's like I've been living with both your parents instead of just your mother all these years.

"Do you know what it's like to lie in bed and comfort

somebody you love and cherish as she cries on the anniversary of her husband's disappearance? Or to spend endless hours listening to the woman you care most about in the world talk incessantly about how she fell in love with the father of her child. It's not easy! You should try loving someone whose whole heart and soul belongs to somebody else. You can't fight a memory, or confront a dream. That's what I had to live with all these years. And yet, on top of it all, your mother is everything to me. I would sacrifice anything for that woman."

Jamie was silent.

"I made sure your father was buried properly in a veteran's cemetery, full honours, out of respect for your mother. Everything was taken care of. If you want, you can tell her the truth, but you should know that I didn't hide the truth out of selfishness. I did it to save your mother." Kathryn was drained, emotionally and physically. A huge cross had lifted off her shoulders and now she was fearful of what the immediate future might bring. "Jamie, let her live her life in hope. I'm sure there's a thousand psychiatrists out there who would disagree, but screw them. It's worked for her for the last twenty years. She's happy and the passing time means nothing to her. Let her, and, Galen be."

Trying to avoid eye contact with either of them, I started counting spaghetti noodles splattered across the table. I had gotten into my second dozen when Jamie broke the silence with a logical question.

"There's something I don't understand here. What do you get out of all this? If all my Mom's talk about my father hurts you, why put up with it?"

Kathryn fairly shouted her answer back at Jamie. "Because I need her! She's everything to me. Can't you see, I've invested my life in Patricia. I was there when she needed a friend, it's my turn now. It's my turn to need her."

"Why do you need her?" Jamie said.

"I belong here. We belong together. This is my home now and I want to—"

"It's not your home. It's mine, and Mom's. You don't belong here."

Kathryn grabbed Jamie's coat, pleading. "Jamie, I love your mother. If you tell her about the telegram, she'll never forgive me. I can't stand to lose another one, to be alone again...."

"My mother isn't 'another one.' She's my mother and this is my father." He shrugged her loose and turned to leave the kitchen.

Kathryn cried, "Where are you going?!"

"To have a talk with my mother," was all he said.

Pushing him aside she sprinted for the hallway. "Don't! Please don't!"

She disappeared down through the kitchen doorway with Jamie not far behind, his booming voice chasing after her: "Get away from that door!"

Then, from the kitchen, I heard a rustling and banging, then a door slamming. Voices rising and falling, in anger and fear, were pouring out of that room.

I could smell the garlic bread from the oven beginning to burn. I fished it out, and then on reflection took an unburned slice and left the house. Once outside I drank in the taste of both the bread and that beautiful sunset disappearing over the islands at the far end of the lake. The heat lightning had disappeared and it was time for me to go home.

Behind me, I heard the shattering of glass—probably the window we had put in yesterday.

The Man Who Didn't Exist

Technically, Jimmy Pine doesn't exist. That's a hard trick to pull off when you're six feet, two inches and tip at least 230 on the scales. But still, there's no record of his birth, life or existence on file anywhere in this country.

Within the confines of the Otter Lake Reserve, Jimmy is as well known as a friendly dog, and just as amiable. But when you cross the borders of the Reserve and venture into Lakefield or Peterborough, the federal, provincial and municipal governments regard him as a persona non-grata, an invisible man, which suits his family just fine.

I know all this because I'm his cousin, though you couldn't prove it legally. Jimmy Pine is one of our village's biggest secrets.

Years and years ago, so long back that people don't like to remember that far, Jimmy's mother, a wonderful woman named Greta Pine lost two children. Not to disease or death— that would have been easier to accept than the reality of what happened. Greta Pine lost her children to the institutions of the greater civilization which called itself Canada.

Greta's first born, a chubby little boy she and her husband Karl named Moses, was appropriated into the Residential School system, as was the custom at the time. At the tender age of eight, Moses disappeared. Moses was one of the thousands of Native children who went into the bureaucratic/religious laundry that took an entire generation of Native children through the wash, rinse and spin cycle and then hung them out to dry. Many, including Moses, fell from the clothesline.

Greta's next child, a beautiful little girl christened Dawn, was scooped up within four months of her birth by the Children's Aid Society. A difficult childbirth had rendered

Greta unable to care for Dawn for several months. Taking this as evidence of an unfit environment, it wasn't long until the government-issued car that many Native parents learned to fear appeared in Karl's driveway, then left, bearing a new passenger.

The Powers That Be were notoriously tight-lipped about the journey and destination of the children under their jurisdiction. So, like her brother before her, Dawn soon faded from the world of Otter Lake, though never from her parents' hearts and memories.

That left Jimmy, the third and final child, born in 1965, though again, nobody can prove it. According to Greta's midwife, Jimmy was born covered with a caul, a thin membrane left over from the placenta.

It is said by the Elders that when a child is born surrounded by a caul, it is a sign of good things to come. The child has been singled out by the Creator and is destined for great achievements. Of course that's what they used to say, but since most babies have been born in a hospital or health clinic for the last fifty or sixty years, there hasn't been much of an interest in understanding the significance of cauls, especially since the medical establishment takes a more pragmatic view of them.

So, keeping with tradition, Greta kept the caul, carefully wrapped and preserved in a lace handkerchief, stored in a small tin box once used for tobacco. Jimmy once pointed it out to me when we were kids. It stood on the dresser in the far corner of his parents' bedroom. We were both too scared to open it; it was enough just to see the box.

Jimmy confided in me, as only kids do, that his mother had told him he was destined to do something wonderful and great for his people. And that once he had fulfilled his destiny, he was to take the caul and bury it under the biggest, most beautiful pine tree he could find, returning it to the earth from whence all people had sprung.

On reflection, that was a hell of a responsibility to live up to for a kid who didn't exist.

According to family legend, Jimmy's prophetic birth and the two lost children drove Greta and Karl to their fateful decision. Determined to keep Jimmy at all costs, the Pines conspired to keep the birth of Jimmy a total and complete secret.

Under normal conditions this would have been a difficult, even an impossible task, but as has often been said before, Otter Lake is seldom in a normal situation. The village is a community with relatives and extended family in all levels of the bureaucracy of the Reserve.

The plight of Greta and Karl was no secret to the rest of the village. Many on the Reserve had lost children, brothers, sisters, to both the C.A.S., and Residential Schools, and the other institutions of the superior nation, so there was little prompting needed to enlist help.

When Jimmy was little, his parents kept his hair long and uncut. Up until the age of about seven or eight, he could have as easily passed for a little girl as for a little boy. When he went in for his medical check-ups, either to an unaware white nurse on the Reserve or an over-worked doctor in the city, Greta and Karl made sure they had the birth certificates of their two older children handy, just in case.

Jimmy's aunt, the first Native teacher on the Reserve, doctored a few papers and forms to slip Jimmy into the class. After grade four, all the other kids were bussed off the Reserve to a school in Lakefield. Not Jimmy. His aunt, on Greta's request, took over private tutoring and he received as good a high school education as any person who actually existed.

The Reserve's back roads were where Jimmy learned to drive, unseen by the Ontario Provincial Police or the Mounties. Later, when the Reserve got one of its own cops, a Native Special Constable, he was Jimmy's older cousin Tim.

Luckily, because of the extended family to which Jimmy belongs, he was never at a loss for I.D. when he really needed it. For instance, he bought everything he needed in Peterborough, making sure it was tax exempt with his cousin Terry's status card.

One time, though, he came close to being caught. It was at Charley's, a bar in Peterborough, where he and I and a group of friends were hanging out, listening to a typically mediocre country rock band, where he saw her.

Marnie Benojee was her name. And, as luck would have it, she was one of the few people on the Reserve who Jimmy wasn't directly related to—at least not within the last handful of generations. Sleek, still thin, with long black hair that swayed with the barely rhythmic beat of the band, she was sitting three tables to the right of the non-existent Jimmy.

Jimmy had long had a crush on her, or rather her smile, if you listen to his version of the story. Over the years he had watched her go through a handful of relationships, one short marriage and the birth of a baby girl, Zoe. Marnie knew Jimmy's name and had often talked with him at Pow Wows and other social gatherings. But that was the extent of their affiliation.

But that night she sat barely fifteen feet away. And beside her, holding her hand, was Roger Ames. Unfortunately, Marnie had miserable taste in men, and Roger lived up to the standard of his predecessors. Roger was one of those white guys everybody knew by reputation but didn't want to know personally. No doubt he was in Charley's because he had been kicked out of practically every other bar in the city (except maybe for the one gay bar in town and there was little chance he'd be seen dead or alive in that establishment).

I remember that a really bad version of Bob Seger's "Old Time Rock And Roll" was being attempted by the band. With a wild yell of delight Roger jumped up, half dragging Marnie though a dozen crowded tables to the dance floor.

Jimmy's eyes never left them as they started to dance. Who knows why people fall in love with people they barely know. All I know is that I was sitting right beside the poster boy.

The fourteen or so beers Roger had downed hadn't helped his coordination. He was banging off people like a pinball in the hands of an expert. Marnie tried to keep up and keep him up but it was a losing battle. Finally, he bumped into this other guy once too often. Words were said, then more words, quickly getting louder, eventually drowning out the beat of the band.

It wasn't long before the other guy went sailing across a table crowded with beer bottles. His friend stepped in and, well, there went the evening. Bodies were thrown, punches tossed, glass and wood shattering everywhere.

I wanted to dodge for the door, both for my safety and Jimmy's, since I knew the police were probably being called at that very moment. But I spotted Jimmy making his way to the dance floor, using his height and weight to cut a path through the chaos. He wasn't an especially violent person, so this didn't make sense. Then I saw his destination.

At the far corner of the dance floor, Marnie was trapped. Her back was to a railing while the mayhem in front of her kept her cornered.

Like a bulldozer, Jimmy cleared a passage to her, leaned over the railing and lifted her from the dance floor and over the railing like she was a basketball. At first she was startled, then she saw it was Jimmy. I could see him mouth the words "come on" and throw a protective arm around her.

Unfortunately, Roger saw this too. Roger climbed his way up the railing and flung himself onto Jimmy's back. Roger was the smaller of the two, but he had the advantage of surprise and position. He started flailing away at Jimmy, who finally threw him off with a stout elbow to Roger's midsection.

It was then doors were thrown open and the police arrived, just as I'd predicted.

The party ended with Marnie and most of the other woman from the bar being let loose while the majority of the guys were hauled down to the police station. Riding in the police van, we started the complicated matter of preserving Jimmy's invisible status. Over the years, his unique station had become a thing of honour for the community and it was an ongoing joke and a matter of pride that everyone tried to sustain at any cost.

In handcuffs, Paul Gunn, another cousin, managed to slip

Jimmy his wallet full of I.D. We were all pretty sure that we would be fined and released, but that they wouldn't clue into the fact that Paul Gunn was actually six years younger than the person carrying his I.D., a noticeable six years. Other than that, the two looked pretty much the same, close enough that a cop processing a half dozen Native people wouldn't look all that closely.

Evidently, we were wrong. The cop at the front desk, a short, fuzzy type guy, had us all lined up with our I.D. in hand, waiting to be examined. He went from one to the next to the next, like a bee with a badge. He took the driver's license Paul had slipped Jimmy and looked long into the picture.

The six of us, not including Roger, who was being processed elsewhere to prevent an embarrassing repeat of the bar incident in police headquarters, held our collective breath. Luckily nobody noticed six Indians not breathing.

The cop looked up into Jimmy's face, a good five inch difference.

"You look shorter in this picture."

Jimmy leaned over to peek at the picture on the licence. "I'd been ill."

Taking his cue, Paul nudged me with his elbow, pushing me into a desk overflowing with paper, knocking over an expensive, if well-used, typewriter. It hit the floor and shattered into several good pieces, as did the silence and my dreams of having a future.

Almost immediately, short and fuzzy slapped the driver's licence back into Jimmy's hand and made his way towards me.

"Hey! What did you just do?!"

Typically, Paul nodded me a "job well done, cuz," smile.

"It was an accident."

I don't think he believed me.

Four hours later we were released. I now owed the government my fine as well as the inflated price of what they called a practically new, state of the art typewriter.

Ironically, Paul also received a larger fine for not carrying proper I.D. I claimed he was my brother, and since most of us had the same last name, it wasn't difficult to convince the men in blue. As we left the station, Jimmy tossed Paul back his wallet.

"Thanks."

"It was worth it, to get the last laugh."

As we walked to our cars at four in the morning, we all had that last laugh, poorer, but safe again.

Two days later, Jimmy came across Zoe, Marnie's daughter, sitting at the end of Marnie's long driveway, crying. When she saw the big man getting out of his truck, the four year old dove into the ditch and crawled into a culvert. She almost made it in too, before Jimmy grabbed her leg.

She kicked and screamed and did everything she could to get away from Jimmy, and as big as he was, it's a proven fact that it's almost impossible to hold a four-year-old who doesn't want to be held.

But like I said before, Jimmy is a big man. To calm her down, he gently took her head in his hands and stared directly into her eyes. "Zoe, it's me, Jimmy. I'm a friend of your mother's. It's okay. It's all right. Where is your mother? What's wrong?"

All she could do was scream some more and point to her house and a Dodge pickup sitting at the top of the driveway. Marnie didn't own a truck, but Roger Ames did. Faintly, across the long driveway separating the road from Marnie's home, Jimmy heard yelling, a man's harsh bark...then breaking, something breaking.

Immediately, he picked up Zoe and placed her in his truck. "Stay here." He kissed her forehead and shut the door.

Jimmy never told me or anyone else what happened next. But that day, people along the main drag of the village reported seeing the Sodge pickup, one window smashed, make its way rather quickly out of the Reserve and out of Marnie's life.

That was five months ago. Two months ago Jimmy moved in with Marnie. Yesterday, Jimmy phoned and asked me to meet him here, by the shores of Chemong Lake, under the branches of the largest pine tree in the Reserve.

So there we were. "What's up?"

Jimmy stood with a small box in his hands. He looked at it for a moment. "I need your help. But first of all, I have to bury this."

I recognized the small tin box I had seen fifteen years before, and the legend came flooding back from my memory.

"Wait a minute, aren't you supposed to do that after you've done something, like, really great or fantastic? Have you been holding out on me? What did you do this weekend?"

Smiling, he placed the box on a bed of pine needles and began to dig with his hands.

"You know, Marnie and I are kinda serious these days. She needed a good man to love her, and Zoe deserves a proper father. More than anything else in this world, I want to be that person."

"It's kind of obvious, Jimmy. Tell me something I don't know."

Smiling, he opened the box and took out what looked to be an old lace handkerchief. He treasured it in his hands for a moment. "Okay, I will. You know, I've never been really good with women. It's kind of hard to maintain a relationship when you can't go on trips, get a credit card, buy or rent a car or even order cable T.V. So your entertainment possibilities on a date are severely limited. But it doesn't really matter any more. Not with Marnie and Zoe.

"You know that terrific smile Marnie has? The one where her whole face just lights up and you know her spirit is singing? Zoe has that smile too. The great thing, though, is that I can bring it to them, that smile. They've both had some rough years. I think I make them happy. That's important to me."

Jimmy placed the handkerchief and its contents into the ground and slowly covered it with earth. He then smoothed the blanket of pine needles over it.

"You know, to me, I think the best thing I could ever do with my life is take care of Marnie and Zoe. Nothing else in this world could measure up to that. It all seems so right. They're happy, I'm happy. What could be more fantastic and great than that?"

He stood up again, wiping the dirt and needles from his pant legs. "In fact, we want to get married."

Stunned, I could barely utter the obvious: "Jimmy, you can't get married. There's all kinds of paperwork involved and you don't exist, remember?"

He smiled, then winked at me.

"I know, I know. But you have a birth certificate, don't you?"

The White in the Woods

It was Charlie May who first noticed it. He would, because the man has a spectacular row of them in front of his house. And then, over the next three days, Billy Wild, Annette LaBelle and Creek Johnson all woke up one morning to see the evidence. It was happening all across the village and nobody knew why. It was our turn next. Right beside my mother's house stands a low fence comprised of rocks thrown there over the decades by people occasionally trying to farm, or sometimes just to clear the land. Growing amidst that row of stones were two birch trees that decorated that section of our lawn with dappled sunlight.

Both trees were about a foot in diameter, though on the particular morning we woke up, they were a little thinner around the mid-section. Somebody, during the night, for whatever reason, had harvested the bark from the two trees. We were the latest victims in an on-going rash of bark thefts that had left the village trees with their white, mottled, papery strips carefully peeled away from the trunks.

In the olden days, birch bark had a multitude of uses in Native villages, ranging from the obvious and famous canoes, to baskets, to moose callers, to an original artform called birch bark biting where an artist would fold the bark and bite into it at strategic places to reveal in the unfolded bark, something as intricate as a flower, or some other beautiful pattern carefully outlined in the light brown inner bark. But that was a long time ago. Today, very few people use much birch bark, let alone the incalcuable amount missing.

If somebody needed bark, it was customary to ask permission if the tree happened to be on someone's private land. But there was enough of it in the woods, especially out towards the swamp, that this kind of theft seemed unneccesary. So much bark taken so secretly. Nobody knew what was going on. And it bothered them. The people of Otter Lake may love gossip but they hate mysteries.

Typically our Reserve police, who often go weeks between anything exciting happening, like being the security guards at a wedding dance, latched on to the sudden bark disappearances. Before long I found myself being interviewed by Officer Magneen.

"When did you notice the bark was missing?

"Yesterday morning."

"Did you see anything unusual?"

"The bark was missing?"

"Other then that?"

"No."

"Do you know who did it?"

"No."

"Do you know why?"

"No."

"Do you have anything else to tell us that might help us locate the person who did this?"

"Not really".

"Thanks Andrew, see you on Saturday at the ball game." I was shortstop, he was third base.

During the next few days more birch trees showed up in the same stage of undress as the two beside my mother's house, all over the village. About three or four feet above the ground, an incision would be made vertically for about a foot and a half, then the outer bark would be peeled off, leaving the underbark intact. If the harvesting is done during the late spring, as it was now, then the tree has enough time to heal itself before the onset of winter. Evidently whoever was doing this knew what he was doing. The few birch bark peelers still left in our community (who by the way had been thoroughly investigated and their property searched for the hoarded birch bark) said the trees had been properly harvested and had not been permanently damaged.

All in all, about thirty-six harvested trees had been

counted, not including whatever ones might exist deep in the woods or in the less travelled areas of the village.

A week passed, then two, and the reports of missing birch bark began to trail off. Two possibilities came to my mind. The mysterious bark fetishist had accumulated enough bark for his purposes or, possibly, the Phantom of the Forest had exhausted the in-town supply and had moved on to harvesting trees in other parts of the sparsely populated Reserve.

Talk and conversation about the subject ebbed and flowed over the next few weeks, until it had exhausted itself like a grass fire. The summer wore on, and more interesting topics quickly took over, like the Otter Lake Fishing Derby—an annual event that tested the local fishermen's manhood (which was rapidly becoming an irrelevant concern since about a quarter of the participants were now women). But the motto of the Derby remained: "It's not how big your rod is, but how you cast it. And what kind of line do you use."

Somewhere in the midst of the three dozen high-tech boats and equipment was my ten horsepower outboard, suffering from terminal tuberculosis judging by its cough, attached to a standard aluminum boat. I felt somewhat inadequate about my skill, but my mother loved fish and I wanted the prize money. Two thousand dollars and a new outboard—I was willing to kill fish for that.

Most of my friends were also out on the lake that hot August day; William, Paul, Jimmy and a host of others. We had all been out fishing together numerous times, but today we were solitary warriors, sitting in our metal mounts, ready to wage war with fishing tackle.

The Otter Lake Reserve is bordered on two sides by a large lake system, logically called Otter Lake. Sprinkled with innumerable islands and bays dotting the landscape, every family, every individual, has a favourite fishing spot where the biggest and tastiest bass or pickerel could be found. Or, if lucky, a monster of a muskie to test your resolve. So, like ripples leaving a dropped pebble, the three dozen boats scattered across the lake in search of game.

I hung near the shore, heading east towards a bay my father used to take me fishing in, when he was healthy. It was about twenty minutes by boat—thirty the way the dinosaur I was riding in cut through the water. I had neither the natural aptitude, nor the inherent knowledge of how fish think, to guide me. Instead, I had only my father's assurance that this particular bay would get the family a new outboard.

I could see Paul heading across the lake to Snowstorm Island, his usual fishing haunt. Jimmy hung out near the weed patch across from his grandfather's place. William had long disappeared to his "secret" destination. Most of us figured it was a fish market.

Up ahead lay Mukwa Bay, the much promoted location of massive and prize winning fish. Along the shores, trees reached out over the lake, shading the shallow water. This place had always been a favourite spot of mine, one I was kicking myself for not spending more time at. It was remote, the trees were beautiful and lush, the water calm and not chopped up by tourists in speed boats or waterjets. I sat there for a few moments, drinking in the serenity and calmness this place seemed to share. I would enjoy the next couple of hours here. This was a good idea.

I cast my first lure of this perfect day into the water, several dozen feet off shore. It bobbed on the surface, then sank as I reeled it in, hoping it would provide an irresistable attraction for a monster fish. It didn't take me long to get into a Zen state of mind. Cast. Reel. Enjoy Sun. Enjoy breeze. Enjoy day. Cast again. Repeat as necessary. All those hours and money White people spend in therapy had nothing on this. I felt there were no problems in the world.

Somewhere not too distant, I could here a woodpecker doing its thing. It sounded close, and as an idle game, I tried to find it between casts, scanning the woods along the shoreline. I tried to remember what kind of wood they preferred to look for their tasty insects in. I remembered once discovering a nest of woodpeckers in a hollowed out cedar tree but that didn't count. That was a nest, and cedar is a soft wood. It's easier to build a nest in soft wood then in maple or oak. Woodpeckers are not stupid animals.

Due to the soft summer breeze, my boat eventually drifted closer to shore and the busy woodpecker. It was hard to see the actual trees because the sun was shining so brightly that they were hiding in their own shade. But something in the dimly lit line of trees caught my attention. Evidently our bark-napping friend had been here. Knowing what I was looking for, I tried to see deeper into the woods, even scanned the hill-shaped drumlin that created the shore of the bay. There were more birch trees—almost all of them had been harvested.

I thought about the mystery a bit, but the breeze and the sun pulled it away from me. If it puzzled me enough, I could think about it tomorrow. I had a fishing derby to win, and obsessing over birch bark wouldn't help me do that. I forced my mind back to more productive thoughts. Deciding to move further into the bay, I used one of the paddles to move the boat, figuring the engine would only have ruined the placidness of the place.

I found a place near dead center of Mukwa Bay and remembered spending hours in this exact spot with my father years ago, fishing and talking. Sometimes not talking. Just being. I would sit at the front of the boat, and he would sit at the back. We would face each other, cast to opposite sides, and share our lives. Feeling nostalgic, I crawled to the front of the boat, assumed my childhood position, cast my lure and watched it arc far overhead, the sun reflecting off it, silhouetted against the lush green background of the woods surrounding me.

Except is wasn't all green. My eye had caught something buried in the wall of foliage. Barely hearing the plop of the lure hitting the water, I tried to refocus my eyes on whatever had grabbed my attention. It took a second or two to locate it again but there it was, halfway up the drumlin, almost totally hidden by the trees. It was a patch of white. A large patch but I couldn't tell how large. I didn't remember it being there as a child, and something about it looked unnatural. It was too big to be a birch tree, and this was the wrong geography for any type of white rock of that size, especially halfway up a drumlin, a leftover from the glacial age.

I moved the boat around trying for a better view but I only succeeded in loosing the mysterious image entirely. I returned to the center of the bay and there it was again, high up the hill, almost a beacon. Nobody could see it except me, in this specific spot. This time I could discern another odd disturbance in the seeming stillness of the bay. Dogs barking. A lot of them. And it was coming from the direction of the white patch.

When you spend your entire life growing up in a rural area, you tend to know where everybody lives and the places where everybody doesn't live. This was one of those latter places. Behind the drumlin was an old dirt road, once used by loggers, that connected to the larger road near Japland, another sparsely settled part of the community. Other then that, the place was deserted, used only occasionally for camping or fishing. Dogs and large white patches should not be littering the drumlin.

There was a silent thirty second debate raging in my head between greed and curiosity. Two thousand potential dollars versus an explanation of a large white spot and the dogs. It seemed an odd toss-up until I realized the two were not mutually exclusive. Mukwa Bay and the fish would still be there after I took care of my curiosity. I estimated a good thirty minute hike up the side of the drumlin to the location of the white patch, and probably about twenty minutes to get back to the shore. Or possibly three minutes, providing I didn't watch my step on the way down. That would leave a good half day to reel in Moby Dick.

I tied the boat to a large weeping willow overhanging the water. Making my way through the trees, I found what looked like an easy route up the side of the tear-shaped drumlin. I was still a fair distance from my destination when I noticed a third disturbance in how things should be in Mukwa Bay. The first had been visual, the second auditory, the third was odorous. There was a vicious, horrible stench coming off the side of this hill—the closer I got, the worse it got.

It wasn't from the dogs I had heard—I knew that smell well enough. It reeked of what I had always thought biblical brimstone would smell like. I was beginning to have second doubts about the need to satisfy my curiosity. Perhaps whatever is up at the top of this hill had a reason for being out here in the middle of nowhere, smelling the way it did, surrounded by the sound of a dozen dogs or so.

Unfortunately I had waited too long in my indecision. Judging from the growl behind me, one of the dogs I had been hearing for the last half hour had, in fact, found me before I could find it. It was a small mongrel of no definable heritage, the breed common on many Reserves. But what it lacked in size, it seemed to make up for in temperament. And teeth. It growled, barked gnashed its fangs at me. Making a strategic withdrawal, I backed up the drumlin, keeping my front to the dog as much as possible, because basic military strategy dictates it's better to have the higher ground, and make the enemy advance up the hill towards you.

This, however, meant I found myself backing onto a small plateau or shelf in the drumlin, and directly into the heart of the mystery. And more dogs. Lots more.

I lost track after at least fifteen mutts of all shapes and sizes swarmed me, running, jumping and barking all around. I felt like a covered wagon surrounded by Indians in one of those old time Westerns. One black and white dog lunged in and nipped at my pant leg. This was rapidly turning out to have been a bad idea. What was more frustrating was that I had passed up a perfectly quiet day on the water for this scene from Hell, brimstone included.

"G'jih!"

Either God had spoken, in Ojibway, or there was somebody else on this drumlin with me. Over my left shoulder a chunk of wood came flying into the pack of dogs. It hit a grey one making him dart off into the bush with a yelp that made the other dogs scatter. Apparently God had a great overhand throw.

I turned to see the source of this divine intervention. Instead, blotting everything else out, I confronted a wall of white birchbark—more than a wall, almost a mountain face. It was huge, about thirty feet long, and twenty feet high, tied to a framework that looked surprisingly familiar in structure, almost like the keel of a boat. It was all neatly patchworked together, the squares from various sized trees, with different shades and varying textures, all sewn together to be... whatever it was. And off to the side, was a mound of unused birchbark, again almost twenty feet high. So this was the home of the Phantom of the Forest.

Standing not fifteen feet away from me, wearing dirty overalls, no t-shirt, work boots and a rash of mosquito bites was the Phantom himself. Not quite as dauntin as you would expect. He smiled, showing an equally splendid patchwork of teeth.

"Pretty, isn't it?"

I recognized him then, underneath the dirt and the sweat. He was from Otter Lake, and was distantly related to some distant relatives of mine. Duanne.... Something. Duanne North. That was it. I'd seen him, even talked with him a few times while I was growing up. He'had helped teach Sunday School the few times I went. During the long winter months in Otter Lake, your options of things to occupy your time were rather limited. Both his parents were well known for their religious fervour. In fact, Duanne's father had been the lay minister for the village a number of years ago. Everybody had always expected Duanne to follow in his father's footsteps.

But Duanne had problems of his own. A minister is supposed to minister to his flock, but I remember somebody once telling me that Duanne didn't like being surrounded by people. It made him claustrophobic. As more and more people in Otter Lake had more and more children, resulting in more and more houses being built, he felt increasingly uncomfortable. Add to that the sudden influx of Bill C-31 people, Duanne felt compelled to move farther and farther out into the bush. And at one point, I'd heard he'd disappeared somewhere out west in the wide open spaces. Evidently he was back, ministering to his congregation of dogs. And stealing birch bark.

"Andrew's your name, ain't it?" I nodded, but my attention was still on what literally was a vast wall of birch bark. It was mind boggling, not just the fact that nobody in the world had ever seen anything remotely like this to the best of my knowledge, but the obvious amount of work that had gone into it, for whatever mysterious reason. "Sorry about the dogs, we don't get many visitors up here. They won't bother you no more."

He chuckled to himself before following my gaze to what I assumed was his handiwork. "I was hoping to keep it a secret until it was finished but I guess with something this big, this glorious, somebody was bound to find out. What do ya think?"

I could see the stitching that connected every single section of bark with every other section, and in some places, a form of tar or paste that had been used to seal the stitching, making it watertight. It was looking more and more like a huge birch bark canoe. But it couldn't be.

"What is it?"

Smiling proudly, almost glowing with pride, Duanne formed the words slowly. At first I wasn't sure I'd heard properly. "It's a what?"

"An ark."

An immense, enormous, incredibly big, birch bark ark, out in the middle of the woods. I asked the only logical question. "Like the one in the Bible? That ark?"

He wiped his hands on his stained overalls, the way a workman does when surveying his accomplishments. "Yep. My ark. Still got a ways to go yet, be another year or two, but every flood starts with a raindrop."

"You built an ark?!"

"It's hardly an ark yet. Wouldn't float worth a damn right now, but give me enough time and she'll ride out any flood.

Took me a while to figure out how to make it strong and hold up. It's all in the bracing, eh?"

"You built an ark?!"

"That's what I said. My ark."

I couldn't say anything more. What more was there to say, standing there in front of a birch bark ark. Nice ark?

"Want some tea?"

"Um, sure."

He went over to the an old wood-burning stove he'd evidently carried up and left outside for just such an emergency. He put the kettle on the top and checked to make sure there was enough wood still burning in it. I just stood there, looking at the birch bark ark.

Duanne cleared some bark shavings off two stumps near the stove. "Hey Andrew, come over and sit a spell. How's you mother and father?"

"Fine." One syllable words seemed so innocuous in front of that wide expanse of white.

"You still go to Church?"

"No. Not much."

He smiled and gazed at the world around him. "Me neither but I figure you don't need a building of brick and wood to worship God. He's everywhere. He can hear me atop this small mountain as well as any church, huh?"

I swallowed, not really knowing how to reply. "I guess."

There was silence. I could hear the dogs wandering back into the camp. But this time they seemed a little more respectful of me and kept their distance.

"Not much of a talker, are you boy?"

"You're building an ark?!"

"And when you do talk, you repeat yourself. I admit its not something you see everyday, but that's no reason to be anti-social. Sit and talk a while. You're the first one up here to see my little project. How'd you find me?"

Finally I managed to take my eyes off the thing and focus on Duanne North. "From the bay. You could see something big and white in the woods. I got curious."

He looked out towards the bay but all you could see was intermittent spots of blue though the leaves. "Figures—the trees are a might thin in that direction. I picked this spot because I thought it would give me a bit of privacy to finish my little project, but no place is perfect. I'm surprised I got away with it this long. God knows its hard to keep a secret in this village. Milk and sugar?"

"Please." Sitting on the stump by the stove gave me a different view of Duanne North's ark. It was hollow, just some rudimentary framing on one side of the interior, but the whole other side was set to be fitted with the remaining birch bark. The scale of what this man had done, and planned to do, was astounding. I couldn't get over it. The Phantom of the Forest was an aboriginal Noah.

"How big is it?!"

"Oh, the usual. Three hundred by fifty by thirty cubits. Supposed to be made of gopher wood but I don't reckon there's much of that around here. So I improvised. Decided to do it the way our grandfathers would have done it. Our people travelled far and wide with birch bark. It seemed only natural for me to use that instead. Doing pretty good so far." He beamed proudly, almost glowing in his accomplishment. Like he said before, it's hard to keep a secret in Otter Lake, especially when you're the one keeping it. There seemed to be an eagerness, almost an anxiousness to share in him, a desire to bask in his achievements.

"What the hell is a cubit? Oh sorry, I didn't mean to swear."

The kettle went off and Duanne proceeded to make our tea while lecturing me in the fine art of ark building. "I was curious about that myself. I'd never heard of a cubit before, except in Church. But in Genesis, it tells you a cubit is the length from the tip of your finger to your elbow. So doing a little calculation, I sort of figured out what it would roughly come to. So the arks' about four hundred and fifty feet long, seventy-five feet wide and forty-five feet high. That sounds about right, don't it?"

"Sounds good to me." That thing was almost five hundred feet long and three stories tall. That was a lot of birch bark. I drank my tea trying to process and understand all that was happening in this little place near the shores of Mukwa Bay. "Why?"

"Why what?

"Why build an ark?"

"I felt like it," he said uncomfortably. That was it. He smiled weakly, absently reaching down and scratching one of the dogs that had come to investigate our tea drinking.

"People do not feel like suddenly building an ark. At least I don't think so. Not in my experience anyways. Now correct me if I'm wrong but hasn't it only happened once before? And if I remember correctly, Noah had the voice of God telling him to do it." I felt a wet nose and slightly chewed ear rubbing against my left hand. Another of Duanne's congregation. "This...thing of yours must have started somewhere."

Without a sound, he undid the straps to his overalls, letting the front drop open. On his chest, above each nipple were two horizontal scars, each of about two inches in length. Duanne looked embarrassed, almost a hint of disgrace in the way he refused to look at the scars.

They looked familiar, like I should know what they were. Then I remembered. He'd gone out west. "Those aren't what I think they are, are they?" He nodded forelornly. They were Sundance scars. A highly religious prairie ritual that involves having wooden pegs pierce the flesh of your chest. These pegs are attached to a central pole and the object is to pray and dance continuously around the pole until they rip out. It's not for the faint of heart. In fact, Duanne was the first person I'd ever seen with the scars. But what was a good Christian boy doing with Sundance scars?

"I strayed." Turning away from me, he did up his overalls again. I could tell those scars were not the badges of honour they were intended to be.

"How...?"

"Because I'm weak. You must have heard I went out West to do some missionary work. While I was there I ran into some people." I didn't like the way he said "some people". "They...I believed them."

"Did they hurt you?"

"No, I hurt myself. I did this. Of my own free will. That makes it all the more...wrong. This was not God's work. I should have known better. I should have guarded myself against the words of false idols. For a while, I believed there was another way, a different, better way. But like the Bible says, God is the only way."

"Duanne, I think you're over...."

"I had to do penance. Make my peace with God for wandering from the path."

"I don't think participating in a Sundance Ceromony is a bad thing. Most people would consider it an act of courage, even piety."

"I allowed myself to believe that. But I have put all that behind me. I am reborn, for there is no other way but the Lord and the Bible. I am forever scarred by my actions, but I might be able to save my soul. By building an ark!"

I was beginning to feel exceedingly uncomfortable. It's one thing to believe in the Bible, my parents do, and to a lesser extent, so do I. But it's another thing to build an ark. And to have tea with the builder. This was not covered in any Sunday School class I ever attended. I am of that generation that was drifting from the beliefs the white institutions had forced upon us, and was now considering what had been believed before the dark times had come. I was hardly fundamentalist in any sense of the word and I was respectful of both belief systems.

It was my turn to sip my tea nonchalantly. "Have you, like, heard God telling you to do this? I mean, have you actually heard a voice or something?"

His attitude changed and he laughed out loud, scaring the dog away. "You mean burning bushes type thing? No, nothing like that. I'm just a simple man. But I hear my duty inside me.

"You should build an ark," it said. I was meant to create this ark, I know this, and if I keep up the pace I've set, I should have it finished a couple months before the millennium."

"The millennium? What does the millennium have to do with anything?" This was beginning to get way over my head.

"Don't you pay attention to anything! The millennium! It's all part of the whole big picture. Great and wonderful things are expected to happen. Serious and fantastic things happen every thousand years. Somebody once estimated that Creation happened in 4004 B.C. Practically a millennium, if they had them back then. The Great Flood happened five thousand years ago. More recently, Jesus Christ, our Saviour, was born two thousand years ago, and a thousand years later the Mayan civilization died out. I think we're due for another flood, especially with this El Niño thing I keep hearing about. And Andrew, I think Native people are the chosen people!"

"Otter Lake people?"

He nodded confidently. "Yes. And what better way to redeem yourself then by saving Otter Lake! The rains should start on January first and everybody here can sail away in my ark. Now there's a hell of a way to get out of Hell, wouldn't you say?" He paused for a moment, a look of thought crossing his face. "Though January's a hell of a time to be out on the water."

Duanne finished his tea before getting up. "Sorry, got to stir my tar. Excuse me." I couldn't help wondering if Noah had been this polite. He half waddled half scurried over to another large circular fireplace a dozen or so feet from the ark. Over it was a large pot, almost a caldron, boiling away. He picked up a large paddlelike object and began stirring it. "If you're not careful, the whole thing will boil away and harden. I've had that happen a few times already, I get so caught up in my work. Can you pass me that bucket over there, please?"

The bucket was near the pile of unused birch bark, down wind of the fire. I fetched it for him and immediately my eyes stung and watered so badly I almost dropped the bucket. Whatever I had smelled earlier down the drumlin was emanating from the cauldron. And however noxious it was a quarter of a mile away, it was beyond belief a dozen feet away. I coughed and ran around the fire as fast as I could trying not to spill the contents of the bucket. "You get used to it after a while, but it sure clears out your sinuses, don't it?"

I didn't trust myself to answer without rapidly emptying my stomach. Instead I handed him the bucket and watched him through tear stained eyes pour some of it into the larger pot. "The dogs love it though. That's how they all ended up here. They can smell this concoction miles away. I know I'm supposed to have two of everything but what the hell, I like dogs." The viscous goo pouring out of the bucket smelled familiar, like concentrated pine. "Pine gum" he said. "Some pine gum, bear fat and some wood ash and a few other odds and ends will seal this thing tighter than a duck's ass. Old family recipe. You think finding enough birch bark was hard, try finding enough bear fat. It don't grow on trees, you know."

"You're doing this all by yourself? At least Noah had a family to help."

"Most of my family don't talk to me much. I like to think these dogs are my family but they sure don't help me much either. Just bark and run around a lot. Actually, they are a lot like my real family" With that, he let out a hearty laugh. Taking a large spoon, he reached into the caldron and scooped up a large piece of bear fat that hadn't been rendered yet, and threw it at the dogs. Four of them scrambled to swallow it in a frenzy of barking. "Got to be careful to pick a piece that the pine gum hasn't touched. They hate boiled pine gum. Come to think of it, I'm not to particularly fond of it myself." He laughed again.

While still stirring, he shared his most serious expression of the afternoon. "I suppose you think I'm crazy? Building an ark like this?"

"No. No, not at all. It pays to be prepared I guess."

"Wanna help?"

With those words, I could see a look of hope, or friendship being expressed, an olive branch being extended. It was a big job, huge in fact. He definitely needed help. But I couldn't help looking at the reality of the situation. He was building an ark for an up-coming flood, here in the woods of Mukwa Bay. I believe in religious tolerance, even in preparing for the future, even in Murphy's Law, but this went beyond everything one could fit into any logical equation. Andrew's Law dictates 'whatever can go wrong, you stay away from.'

"I don't think so. Sorry Duanne. I've got other obligations"

Disappointment spread across his face. Apparently he had held serious hope I would join him in his venture. More hope than a knowledge of reality. "I guess it is a lot to ask. Thanks anyway, Andrew. I guess I'm supposed to finish this myself. But you will keep it a secret huh? Please? I mean, I'll tell everybody when the time comes, that's why I'm building it. Just not right now. And I will need a lot of help later on, to go off to the zoo to get all the other animals we'll need. You know everybody who owns a pickup truck, don't you Andrew?"

Offering as much assistance as I could without promising anything concrete, I left Duanne North, high on the drumlin with his ark. A couple of dogs followed me down to my boat before becoming bored or convinced I had no food. I spent the rest of the afternoon sitting in our family boat, pretending to fish. I would cast, then fifteen minutes later remember to reel the lure in. I had a few nibbles but nothing struck with any real interest. All the time, I could see the white surface shining out from beneath the green foliage.

I went home without two thousand dollars or a new motor. As I motored my way along the shoreline home, it surprised me how many white or light coloured houses lined the green shores of Otter Lake. I had promised Duanne I would keep his secret. And I would. Part of me did it out of respect for Duanne's dream, the other, more evil part was curious to see what would happen on January 1, 2000, when Duanne unveiled his birch bark ark to Otter Lake.

During the next few weeks, whenever I found myself near Mukwa Bay or Japland, I vainly tried to see if I could detect any evidence of something white proudly announcing its presence in the forest. But the ark was too well camouflaged, hidden too far back in the woods to be seen from civilization. Its secret held. In my mind's eye I could see it growing, getting bigger, taking form. I estimated Duanne might have two thirds of one side done by now. Still a long way from completing it, but probably becoming more than just a dream—each day coming closer to being a reality.

Then came late September. I was taking the shortcut through Japland to a nearby small town to pick up some groceries for my mother. All along the sides of the road the birch bark trees had been harvested, the bands of black indicating where Duanne North had tapped the resources of Mother Nature to do the bidding of God. Hopefully Duanne had gotten himself enough to continue his work over the winter. Come the spring, I had a feeling Duanne would be finding himself wandering farther a field in search of more raw materials.

At one point, the road climbs halfway up another drumlin, cutting though the crest, revealing to the driver a wonderful, if momentary, vista of the surrounding area. One of the prettiest spots in the village, I often stopped there to enjoy the view. But this time it was marred by a large black cloud rolling out of the forest, about three miles west of the road. There had been no thunderstorms with lightning to start fires, and nobody I knew lived out that way. Towards Mukwa Bay. Except Duanne.

Fearing the worst, I jumped back in my car and headed toward Joplin's Turn, the nearest spot a car could get to Duanne's camp. Still, the Turn was over two and a half miles away from the drumlin and it took almost an hour before I reached the ark. Or what was left of it.

The wood bracing still stood, charred and burned, totally useless, but the bark itself had burned away. The air hung heavy with the aroma of burned wood and bear fat/pine gum/wood ash tar. The ground was littered with little fires, errant pieces of birch bark that had flown off the main conflagration, trying to eat up the damp pine needles that carpeted the camp. All the trees, both in the camp and surrounding it, especially down-wind, showed evidence of being scorched. Luckily it had been a wet summer or the fire would have been more biblical in proportions.

The camp seemed deserted. "Duanne! Duanne!" There was no answer. Not even from the dogs. I ran through the camp, checking his cabin, and forced myself to quickly check the ashes of the ark. Nothing, thank God. There was no sign of Duanne.

He had said earlier that no burning bush had talked to him. I wondered what a burning ark, a crushed dream would say to a man in the throws of fulfilling a destiny set out for him by God. And what that man might do when the dream was destroyed. Conceivably by God. Luckily, the options that went through my mind were considered a sin, therefore out of the question for Duanne.

No matter how well watered the forest was, I still felt it prudent to stamp out the multitude of little blazes that peppered the area. It gave me time to figure out what had happened here, and to Duanne, the ark builder. Maybe he had gone into town to get help. It was a long way to go but it seemed the only logical possibility. I had trampled about eight small fires before I heard the gasping and huffing of a near exhausted man coming up the drumlin.

Emerging from the bush Duanne arrived, carrying two buckets of water from the lake. He stopped when he entered the camp, his heaving breath the only sound. It was too late. A matter of too much fire, too little water—too much time had elapsed. His buckets fell from his hands and overturned, draining into the soft pine carpet.

"It's gone. All gone." He fell back on his behind sending up a small shower of burnt birch bark, still staring at the scorched remnants.

"Duanne, what happened?"

"It burned up."

"I know that. How?"

He picked up a half burned piece of birch bark, held it in his hands, eventually crushing it in frustration. It trickled down his hands, the ashes flowing away gently, caught in the fall breeze.

"Duanne?"

"The dogs. They did this."

I looked around but there were still no dogs in the area. "The dogs?! Duanne, how could they do this? Talk to me Duanne."

Duanne got to his knees, then his feet. Walking almost blindly, he approached his life's dream. He seemed to talk without choice or effort. The words came out like on automatic pilot. "The tar. They wanted the bear fat in the tar. They upset the pot. The fat caught fire. And my ark..." His voice trailed of and he stood directly under the huge remaining timbers that made up the frame of the ark. "My ark..."

Then suddenly, he grabbed an unused plank from the ground and started pounding the side of the support beam. He hammered and pummelled it, sending off nuggets of burnt wood and sparks flying across the camp. One caught in his hair but he didn't notice as it sizzled, then went out, all the time yelling out, "Why? Why? Why?" The whole thing was shaking from the force of his pounding. It rocked back and forth, wobbling. I could see chunks of half burnt wood fall to the ground but Duanne was too busy venting his wrath to notice.

But I could also see the all to obvious signs of structural weakness, burnt-through beams and support planks charred to cinders. You'd have to be blind, or crazed with rage, not to. "Duanne, don't do that! That thing will..." Several loud cracks drowned out my words as the framework for a four hundred and fifty foot by seventy five foot boat came tumbling down into a mess of partially incinerated wood, on top of Duanne. He disappeared underneath it without uttering a sound.

Some of the wood was still hot and sparks flew everywhere under the collapse. Thinking surprisingly quickly, I used my jean jacket to protect my hands as I threw charred timbers and planks aside in a desperate search for Duanne. It was barely a dozen seconds before I found him, his clothes smoldering on top of some live embers. I did what I could to put them out and pull Duanne from the wreckage. He was still saying, though more softly "Why? Why?..."

He was bleeding from his shoulder and a leg, one hand and the side of his face looked burned, and he had a horrible wheezing sound coming from his lungs. His cries for answers were soon replaced by coughing. In between spasms, he grabbed my shirt, asking again, "Why?"

"I don't know. You can always build another one. I'll help this time." He smiled a sad smile, one that again said too little too late. He laid back in my arms, still smiling.

"It was beautiful, wasn't it?"

"It was amazing."

Duanne looked puzzled for a moment, in thought. Then in a sad, regretful tone, he simply said "hmmm."

"What does that mean, Duanne?"

He had another coughing spasm, this one stronger then the last. When it subsided, he looked calmer. "I was just thinking. What if I misunderstood. What if I was suppose to build a park, instead of an ark. Maybe that's why he destroyed it. What do you think? Or am I still being punished?" He give me one last confused searching look. "This hill would have made a nice park, you know." Then his eyes closed.

I left him up there with his ark. Though it was probably illegal, and possibly unethical, I buried him on the side of that drumlin, hoping he'd found his redemption. I'm ashamed to admit it, but my Bible studies were a little lax, and I'm not sure if Noah was buried on the side of Mount Ararat, the place where the first Ark originally landed. Duanne's ark never even saw a drop of water. It's said fragments of the original Ark can be found atop that mountain, in far away Turkey. But if you're not to picky about your arks, you can still find some relics over in Mukwa Bay.

Ice Screams

It's been three days and I'm still here, sitting in that back corner, away from everyone. Three days.

People are looking at me funny. Most of them were here the first night I came in and are surprised to still see me sitting in the corner when they come back, but I don't care. I just order another drink. But that's why they look at me funny. I'm not known as a particularly hard drinker—in fact, only a handful of people in this bar could claim to have ever seen me drunk once, let along for three straight days.

I know they're all dying to ask me what happened out there on the ice, but that would defeat the purpose of drinking. I'd have to remember.

So instead I sit here, listening to the same country songs played on the jukebox over and over again. If it was a weekend, there would be a band, but not in the middle of the week. The waitress keeps eyeing me warily. I guess years of training have taught her to watch people who power drink. But I won't be a problem. I just want to be left alone, drink some more rye and try to burn some memory cells.

Steve and David came in earlier and joined in, though I made it obvious I was not fit for company. I kinda got the feeling my mother probably sent them to talk sense into me, or at least to keep an eye on me. But Mom knows what happened, and she knows I have to work this out myself, though I doubt she agrees with my methods. But, as everyone knows, fear and alcohol often hold hands.

"If The Drinking Don't Kill Me, Her Memory Will" starts to play. What little feeling I have left tempts me to smile at the irony. Except in this case, it would be "his memory" and it sure as hell isn't a love story.

It's been three days since what happened to Ryan but the

memory still scares the hell out of me, a good four bottles of rye later. The sharp reports from the pool table make me think of my buddy William. Normally he'd be at that table exercising one of the few talents he has in life. I wonder what he's doing now? Probably hiding at home, since he doesn't drink anymore.

Steve and David get up to leave. They've been there a good three hours, keeping an eye on me. They've done their good deed but they have families and work tomorrow. They look at me, then open the door to leave. A cold blast pours in and, in the distance, I can see the multicoloured light of this small town stretching down the street. Steve and David see the numbed look on my face, shudder, then leave.

They'll probably take the 507 to the cut off, then drive across the lake to the village. People have short memories when they're in a hurry. The lake is usually frozen over by this time of year, taking a good fifteen minutes off the trip into town. People from the village always travelled across the lake, even before most people had cars. Years ago, people drove sleighs or even walked across the two mile lake. It was supposedly safe from mid December to early March. But having grown up there, most of the local people can handle the frozen lake. That's what makes what happened to Ryan's parents so puzzling. What happened shouldn't have happened.

It was late February, a safe enough month. There were still some great winter sales on and his parents, always frugal shoppers, decided to go all the way to Toronto to spend four days on a buying binge. It was all planned. Being only nine at the time, Ryan got to go with them while his older sister stayed behind with relatives.

I've been told Ryan was always particularly close to his parents, closer to them than his older sister was. My mother claims it's because he was a difficult birth. Story has it his mother almost died giving birth to him and then he almost died of some respiratory problem a week later. His mother blamed the nursing staff, saying they didn't watch over him enough and then his father accused one nurse of being racist and prejudiced against Indians. You had to know Ryan's parents.

Needless to say, they both survived. Maureen, his mother, liked to say that she refused to even consider dying until she knew if her little one would be okay. That sort of set the pattern for the rest of their lives.

By pattern I mean that he was the baby of the family and was treated as such. It was obvious that he was favoured by his parents but that happens in some families. Of course, that's not to say the parents neglected or didn't love Aricka, his sister. He just always got the benefit of the doubt, or the bigger slice of the pie. Pretty soon Aricka learned to accept this, though it was through gritted teeth. It's amazing that Ryan didn't grow up more spoiled than he really was.

I remember how excited Ryan was about going to Toronto. He'd never been there before. Aricka, fours years older, shrugged off his enthusiasm, a little hurt that she wasn't going. All she had to look forward to was a week of exams and staying with her aunt.

Standing at the school bus stop that morning, all she talked about was her brother and the trip. Minus ten degrees and she could still whine.

"He always gets what he wants. Mom treats him better than me. She always does. 'He's the baby,' she says. If you baby someone all the time then they'll be a baby all the time." I stamped my frozen thirteen-year-old feet in response. The school bus was late, probably due to the heavy-falling snow. The possibility of a day off from school was in all our minds, so we didn't much care about Ryan or Aricka's problems.

All except for William. William Williams was my best friend then and now, and don't ask me why. He could be an idiot sometimes, in fact most times, but I accepted that. It was one of those friendships which defy explanation. Now William had little affection for Ryan. Ryan had never done anything against William or vice versa so there were no real grounds for his dislike. But he hated the attention Ryan got from his parents because William was somewhere in the middle in a family of nine. You had to fight hard for any recognition at his house. I suspect the real reason came from a secret crush William had on Aricka. He would agree with anything she said just to get on her good side.

"It must be terrible having a brother like that," he said sympathetically. He could always be counted on to be sympathetic to a pretty girl when it was necessary, even at that age and temperature.

Aricka watched the family truck approaching through the growing snowfall. "You get used to it. Someday though, he won't always be the favourite. He won't be so hot then. The little scum."

Then the family's Ford came rolling down the street, on its way to Toronto, the family ready to buy out the town and fit as much of it as they could into their beat up old vehicle. It was a yearly thing with that family and a few others on the Reserve. The income tax refund came in early and already it was mentally spent.

The last anybody saw of them was the back of their truck roaring down towards the lake, a trail of snow and exhaust billowing up through the air. I remember Ryan sticking his tongue out at Aricka as they disappeared onto the whiteness of the lake.

Aricka blew into her hands. "I hope they get a flat."

William responded with a hearty "yeah" and smiled like someone who's just scored some victory points.

After that it gets kind of strange.

Three days passed before Mags Magneen noticed a light on at Ryan's house as she was driving by. According to what she knew, they were still supposed to be in Toronto. No car was in the driveway and nobody answered the phone. Always the curious (some would say nosey) type, she decided to investigate.

The way she tells it, the house looked "as cold as a Christian's heart." A blanket of virgin snow surrounded the house. She had to break a trail as she walked up to the front door. The light was still on, but the house "felt" empty as she put it.

A couple knocks on the door went unanswered, as did the harder pounding which followed. Feeling somewhat uneasy, Mags was about to give up and leave, but decided to give it one last try and rattled the doorknob. She discovered that the door was unlocked. Puzzled, she swung it open.

"Martin? Maureen? Are you here? Hello." No answer. She shivered, not sure if it was from the cold or the eerie silence.

The house was cold, colder than outside it seemed. Some of the lights were on, but the place still looked dark. Mags called out a few times but, other than the unnerving echo of an empty house, there was no response. The kitchen was clean as always and Mags was confused. It wasn't like Ryan's family to leave the lights on when they went away, let alone leave the door unlocked. Yet they weren't there and weren't due back for a few days.

She wandered into the livingroom and looked around. Again, nothing looked as if it had been touched in several days, except for the comforter on their big couch. Mags had given it to Ryan's mother four years before. Now it was lying all in a bundle in one corner of the couch.

Mags was beginning to feel the February cold by this time and was tempted to leave, maybe make a few phone calls later on to some relatives, inquiring about the location of the family. Still puzzled over the strange state of the house, she absentmindedly picked up the comforter from the couch and started to fold it.

Ryan looked back at her from under the comforter. Mags screamed and jumped a good six feet back, knocking over a plant and the worn out Lazyboy and ending up against the window. Ryan, his expression never changing, followed her with his brown eyes.

"My God, Ryan, you scared the hell out of me! What are you doing underneath that blanket?"

Ryan nearly looked at her, still not saying anything. "Ryan, are you okay? Where are your parents?" Ryan shivered, picked up the rapidly discarded comforter, and pulled it back over himself. He disappeared back into the couch as quickly as he had appeared.

"Ryan?" Mags tried again. Again no answer. She approached the couch again, more timidly this time, still calling out Ryan's name, with the same lack of response as before. Her gloved hand reached out slowly and tugged at the comforter until Ryan's face and upper body were visible.

"Ryan, what happened to you?" Ryan merely blinked his eyes at her and shivered again.

According to Mags, poor Ryan looked like hell. He was still in the same clothes he had worn when he and the family had driven off the Reserve three days ago. His face held no expression, just a steady blankness, and it was thinner. The doctor later estimated that nine-year-old Ryan had lost six pounds in three days.

A nervous Mags covered Ryan in the comforter and another blanket from the overturned lazyboy. Ryan didn't flinch. You could barely see the little trickle of vapour escaping from his mouth into the cold air. Mags then searched every room in the house, but couldn't find anything that would explain Ryan's mysterious appearance.

In the kitchen, some of the plants were dead from exposure to the cold. A large window overlooking the backyard had been forced open and left that way. Footprints outside the window led from the bushes, away from the lake. They were the same size as Ryan's feet. Mags was beginning to get really scared.

"Ryan, listen to me. Where are your parents? Did they leave you here?" Ryan didn't respond, Instead, he tried to duck under the comforter again. Mags quickly grabbed his arm and immediately let go again. "Your arms are so cold!" Ryan stopped moving for a moment and looked at Mags, his brown eyes both looking and not looking into hers.

"Cold," was all he said.

That was enough for Mags. The police were there in fifteen minutes. Aricka was driven in from school. Uncles, aunts and cousins all converged on that little house, but still Ryan refused to talk. The more they asked questions, the more unresponsive he became. Aricka was getting panicky. At one point she screamed at Ryan to say where their parents were. She had to be dragged out of the room and looked after by the doctor. The doctor then quickly examined Ryan, but it was obvious what was wrong: he was hungry, dehydrated, suffering from hypothermia and shock.

One of the cops followed the footprints as far as the lake, but by then the wind had obliterated any trace of a trail. They later theorized that Ryan had been in the house for the last three days, not eating anything or doing anything, just sitting there under the comforter and occasionally going to the bathroom. That became fruitless after the pipes froze and burst the first night.

"But where are his parents?" Everybody had a good idea as to the answer to this question, but they were afraid to voice it.

It was Mags who took the first step. After some prodding, her husband finally agreed to take two of the Constables out to follow the winter road across the lake.

They were out a little over a mile, travelling slowly and studying the surface intently, when they came across a break in the shallow snow wall which lines the winter road. It was almost invisible, hidden by the three-day-old fallen snow. After that, it wasn't long before they found the remains of a trail—a trail that ended abruptly at a patch of freshly frozen ice.

The police later theorized that Ryan's parents got lost in the thick snowstorm that was falling that morning and veered off the main road towards the channel, where a half mile away, they went through the ice. Somehow, Ryan must have gotten out of the car and crawled onto the safe ice. He liked riding with the back window open because he sometimes got car sick. He must have walked home, soaking wet, through the snowstorm and subzero weather, and then broke into his own home. Three days later he was found. They never found the car, though. The lake is over two hundred feet deep.

Even to this day, a good quarter of the village won't drive

across the lake anymore because of what happened. People say it was just an accident, but you can still see the shudder sweep across their faces when they talk about it, usually around freeze up or melt down. Oh sure, every winter some fool people go through the ice like clockwork. It's usually some white cottagers who decide to go and try their new snowmobiles out on the lake too early or too late in the season. Or sometimes they race across the lake and forget where they're going and drift a little too close to the channel where the ice is thinner because of the current. Kiss the skidoo and the occasional cottager goodbye. Most of the Native people haven't gone ice fishing near the channel since Kid Johnson caught what he thought was a hell of a big fish there one spring.

Eventually they took Ryan to the hospital, and considered taking Aricka too, but one of the aunts convinced the doctor that she could better take care of her. The cops wandered around aimlessly, a little ill at ease and a bit confused. There were no bad guys to chase, no bodies to identify or take away, no tickets to write. All they had were two kids, one pretty well catatonic, and a big hole in the lake. Pretty soon they packed up and left the house to the relatives.

I remember playing in the snow as the cop cars drove by our house. Us kids hadn't heard the news yet, but my parents had. They looked out the window at the retreating cars with sombre expressions on their faces. We knew something was up, but when you have two feet of good snow to play in, who cares.

By that night everybody knew, regardless of age. Contrary to popular belief, not a lot of exciting things happen on Reserves. This event would keep the phone lines tied up for at least a good month. Once the news got around, a bunch of us kids would gather by the shore of the channel and look out towards the section of lake where the car went in, looking vainly for anything out of the ordinary—as if we were expecting the car to come driving out through the ice, or at the very least Maureen and Martin to suddenly appear to a half dozen partially frozen children. Kids are strange people.

Aricka was back in school within three days. Some of her closest friends surrounded her and offered companionship and support, kid style, but the majority of us wouldn't go near her if we could help it. If we bumped into her in the hall we'd say "hello" and all that, but that was the extent of it. For some reason she seemed tainted with something dark and we didn't want to have anything to do with it. William swore off his crush on her, preferring fresh game. I even felt guilty about avoiding her.

But one place I couldn't avoid her was in class. I sat beside her in history. Usually a talkative girl, all day she just stared at her books, occasionally looking up when the teacher spoke. The teachers knew enough not to call on her for any questions, which surprised those of us who doubted the common sense of most teachers. At one point her pencil broke, and she fumbled around in her pencilcase for another. She always liked writing in pencil—said it gave her a chance to rethink things. I offered her mine. I'm a pen type of guy. She looked at me. I think I even caught a bit of a smile.

"Thanks." She took it and went back to work. That was our conversation for the day.

Ryan on the other hand was a different story. He was in the hospital for two weeks, in bad shape. His body temperature was really low and he had other problems. He wouldn't eat. He wouldn't do anything. They even brought in one of those psychiatrists, but with little result. It was like talking to a disconnected telephone.

One day, about a week after my conversation with Aricka, William and I paid him a visit. Actually, that's not quite correct. Rather, my mother, in exchange for a trip into town to see a movie, told William and I that we'd be making a pit stop at the hospital, whether we wanted to or not. It was sort of Mom's Reserve version of home psychiatric treatment. If only dogs can talk to dogs, then only kids can talk to kids.

William was not amused. The last thing he wanted was to spend a Saturday afternoon in a hospital talking to some orphan kid gone crazy that he never liked in the first place. William is like that. To tell the truth, I didn't want to be there much myself, but neither of us could or would say no to my mother.

"I hate your mother," was all William could say as we walked down the antiseptic-smelling snow white hallway. That's how we found ourselves going into room 413—an ominous number if we'd ever heard one.

The door was open and we entered. We could see him from where we stood. Ryan was almost lost in the sheets. We were surprised at how different he looked, how much weight he'd lost. He almost disappeared into the pillow and sheets. Only his dark skin told us where he was.

We shuffled nervously, neither of us wanting say anything in the quiet of that room. There were two other beds there. One was empty and the other had some white kid in it reading a stack of comic books. Ryan seemed oblivious to everything.

Finally I broke the silence. "Hey Ryan, how you doin'?"

The silence returned. William and I looked at each other.

"He doesn't talk. He's kinda spooky." It was the comic book kid, some redhead with a leg in a cast.

"He hasn't said anything at all?"

"Nope. The nurses, the doctors, everybody talks to him but he doesn't say anything. Why's he in here anyway?"

A little more reassured that Ryan wouldn't jump up and grab him, William edged a little closer to him, his curiosity getting the best of him. "His parents went through the ice in a car."

The comic book kid looked surprised. "They put you in the hospital for that?"

"He was in the back seat. Barely got out. I think that's why he's like this." I found myself edging closer. By now we were both at the bedside, looking at Ryan. Seeing all the tubes and medical stuff running everywhere almost made the trip worthwhile.

"Ryan?" No response. "It's Andrew and William."

William managed a feeble "hi." Ryan couldn't manage even that.

"I told you." The comic book kid was getting annoying. William looked at me.

"Well, we tried. Let's go. The movie starts in half an hour."

William was already edging his body towards the door, but for some weird, no doubt morbid reason, I was fascinated by Ryan. I didn't want to leave just yet. "Look at his face. I wonder what he's thinking about. What do you think, William?"

"I don't know. The Flintstones. Let's go."

"He looks cold."

"Not anymore." This time the voice came from Ryan. If it were possible for two thirteen-year-olds to have heart attacks, that was the time. Even the comic book kid looked up in surprise.

"Ryan?!" My voice quivered. Slowly he turned to look at me. The glazed lack of expression had left his face. He now looked like he was either concentrating or constipated.

"I'm in a hospital?"

William and I could only nod.

"My parents are dead, aren't they?"

Again we nodded.

"I'm hungry."

William, still a bit nervous, reached in his pocket and brought out a package of gum. He removed one stick and held out his hand towards Ryan.

"It's all I got." Ryan looked at it for a moment, then reached over and grabbed. The moment his hand touched the gum William jerked his hand away.

"Thanks." Ryan mechanically removed the wrapper and put it in his mouth. The chewing looked like it took some effort. The only noise that could be heard in the room was the sound of gum chewing and comic book pages being turned.

After a moment of silence, Ryan pulled himself up in bed and looked out the window. "So, what's new?"

"Ryan, are you okay?" I always seem to find myself in the

role of the big brother. Ryan still was not looking at us. He was staring into the glaring sunlight.

"Yeah, I guess."

"How come you haven't talked in a week?"

"I don't know. I just kept seeing Mom and Dad in the car, going through the ice. And pretty soon, I didn't want to see that anymore, so I went to sleep."

"But you were awake."

"'Didn't feel like it. Then I heard your voices, like in school, and I remembered I have a test in Math. Mom always liked me doing good in Math." How about that, my Mom was right. Only dogs can talk to dogs.

"Um, that was four days ago."

"Guess I failed, huh?" Then his whole body started to shake, his face contorted and it was obvious what was coming next. The sobs rolled out of him, gradually getting louder and louder till then filled the room. This was gutwrenching, it looked almost painful. Everybody had seen crying before, but this wasn't ordinary. We bolted for the door, grabbed the first nurse we saw and pointed her in Ryan's direction. Then we got the hell out of there. We'd seen enough scary things for the day. Needless to say, we didn't enjoy the movie much.

The next day at school Aricka made a beeline for me on my way in. "I heard you visited my brother yesterday."

After what had happened, crying and all, we weren't sure if this was necessarily a good thing or not. So I tried to play it cool. "Yeah, we dropped by."

"Thanks, he's talking now."

I shuffled my feet. "And crying."

"Yeah, but the doctors say that's good. What did you say to him?"

"Nothing really. Just said hello and talked about how cold he looked. That's all."

Aricka smiled at me. "Well, whatever you did, thank you." Then she leaned over and did the most amazing thing. She kissed me on the cheek. I'd never been kissed on the cheek by a girl before. I'd never been kissed anywhere. It was the strangest feeling I'd ever had. My insides were melting, I would have died for this thirteen year-old-girl, yet I was terrified that someone had seen us. I figured I was too young to die of embarrassment. I just stood there, stunned. And she was still standing there too. "Could you do me another favour?"

Barely trusting myself to talk, I managed to sputter out "What?"

"Help me do something. Come with me out on the lake."

I came to instantly. "Are you crazy? Your parents just...well you know."

"I want to put some flowers on the spot where they...were. I was so mad at them when they left. I'll feel better if I say goodbye. Please come with me."

There was no way I was going to go out on that ice ever in my lifetime, let alone within ten days of what happened. Not for any girl.

"Sure, when?"

She smiled the most incredible smile. "Tomorrow, after school." She kissed me again and went in the school. This set the pattern for the many stupid things I would find myself doing for women over the next dozen or so years.

The next thirty hours were less than enjoyable. The thought of going out onto that ice terrified me. The weather was getting warmer, yet my feet were getting colder. All through school the next day she smiled and gave me the thumbs up. Finally, three o'clock rolled around, as did my stomach.

She was to meet me at the doors of the school. I was half tempted to make a run for it, but I had made a promise. I was scared but proud. The last few students made their way through the doors, then she showed up.

She solemnly buttoned up her coat. "Let's go. We have to stop at my house first."

It was there where she picked up her flowers. She had moved back into the house about a week ago, and one of her unmarried aunts had moved in with her. Somehow she had scammed her aunt into getting some flowers for her, saying they were going to some gravesite. "I'll deal with my aunt later," she said as she gathered them up. This was the first time I'd been in that house since it happened. It was unnerving. Nothing looked changed, except an 8 x 10 picture of the family that had once been a 5 x 7. The smiling eyes of Maureen and Martin seemed to stare out at me. So did Ryan's.

We retraced the steps Ryan had taken from the lake to the house. There was already a path broken in the snow, no doubt created by the cops as they investigated. Aricka was talking on about the state of her family but I couldn't listen. I kept thinking about Ryan walking the entire distance, wet, and a zombie. I shivered from more than the cold. Aricka led the way, her arms full of roses. I followed.

"Ryan's doing good. The doctors say he can come home in a few days. I saw him last night. He misses me, and the family, but he won't talk about Mom and Pop. The doctors say not to force him."

I almost tripped over a buried log and stumbled off the path. In the freshly overturned snow, I saw a flash of red. I picked it up and it was a red mitten of some sort.

"Aricka? What colour were Ryan's mitts?"

Aricka trudged on, without even looking back. "Red, why?"

I threw it away like it was covered in ants. "No reason."

We finally reached the windswept lake. I tried to see the other side but the glare from the snow made me squint. Walking on the ice was a lot easier. The constant wind had packed the snow quite well, giving it a little padding, almost like walking on long grass.

The wind howled at us as I stupidly put one foot in front of the other, wishing I was anywhere but here. Aricka led the way, a good two feet in front of me. I couldn't help but think that if my family knew I was out here, I might as well go through the ice. I tried to look through the blinding glare to make sure nobody could see us, or identify me.

Suddenly Aricka stopped, then I stopped. We had been

walking about twenty minutes and had come to a place where it was obvious a lot of people had been standing around. Cigarette butts littered the area, as well as the odd pee stain. The police had been here. And there, in the centre of everything, was a refrozen jagged blot in the lake. I couldn't take my eyes off of it, knowing that somewhere beneath it, a couple of hundred feet or so, was a Ford with two overweight Indians in it. And they would probably be there forever.

Aricka stood there for a moment. Then she took a deep breath and walked forward. He foot gingerly tested the new ice but by then it had frozen solid enough to support the weight of a thirteen-year-old girl. She walked to the centre of the blot, and kneeled. She put the roses down gently and seemed to pet them for a moment. Freezing, but not wanting to say anything, I shuffled from one foot to another.

"Goodbye, Mom, Pop. I'll remember you." I think she was crying, but I couldn't see because of her coat hood. In the coldness of the wind, I was worried the tears might freeze.

We remained like that for a few minutes before she stood up and started walking back to the shore. Thanking God with every step, I followed.

Without looking at me, she had to shout above the blowing of the wind. "It's over now. Thanks Andrew." Even out on that frigid lake, I felt a little warmer.

Then she stopped and turned around. She had been crying. "I know you didn't want to come, but you did. I knew nobody else would come with me. Or they'd try and talk me out of it. Thanks so much." Then surprise number two happened. She grabbed me and hugged me. I was a little embarrassed, but instinctively my hands went around her. She wasn't still crying or anything, it just felt like she wanted to hold onto something. Out on that barren lake, I guess I was the only thing. After that, we quietly went home.

Ryan came home a few days later, looking more sombre than ever. They had managed to put some weight on him, but he still looked small. Hoping for another hug and kiss I went over to visit them. Ryan almost looked normal, but there was still something about him, something that hovered about him crying out "this kid has seen some seriously scary stuff."

He still wouldn't talk about his parents, or what really happened that day. All the doctors were worried about that but Ryan didn't care. Neither did Aricka. She was just happy to have him back. And to think just two weeks ago, she was calling him "the little scum."

By the summer, Ryan had pretty well become his old self. He was playing with his old friends again, doing things, even laughing. There was a big party on his tenth birthday. I was there, and I even managed to bring William. It was held down at his aunt's place, down near the tip of the lake. After all the festivities had happened, everybody decided to go swimming. The lake was alive with the sound of splashing and laughing kids.

All except for Ryan. He refused to go in the water. He just sat on the dock watching, occasionally waving. But he never went in the water. He blamed it on a cold he had, but there was something more. The fact that he never went swimming, canoeing, fishing, anything water-related ever again, led me to believe I was on to something. Aricka just shrugged it off.

"He'll get over it. Don't worry."

Aricka and I were spending a lot of time together. By the first anniversary of the accident, we were officially an item. Again she talked me into accompanying her out onto the ice, and again we put the roses down, though we had trouble finding the exact spot. We hung out together until we were seventeen, and then the time came for me to go off to college. It was an amiable separation. We just grew apart.

She got a new boyfriend and, every time that anniversary rolled around, she'd drag that poor sucker out onto the ice with her. Same with the one after him. But eventually, a couple of years ago, she married a guy from the Reserve a couple and moved to Peterborough, about a half hour from home.

Ryan did well at school, even became a decent baseball player, but he never left the Reserve for any length of time.

He never had the inclination to go anywhere or do anything. He still lived in his parents' house.

I'd see them occasionally when I came home. I even went out drinking with Ryan a few times. And whenever I wasn't around, William would keep me informed as to what was happening around the village. William was quite happy. He was running the local marina and living with a beautiful woman named Marie. He had everything he wanted, except a charge account at the beer store.

Me, I kicked around the city a bit, doing a little of this, a little of that. I came home every couple of months, though, to recharge my batteries. I finally came home two years ago at the ripe old age of twenty-four. Now I have a steady girlfriend, and an occasional job at the band office, whenever they throw me a contract like somebody throws a dog a bone.

But in my two years back home, I've realized more than ever how true that old saying is: "The more things change, the more they stay the same." The village has a few more houses, a little less forest. In some of the local bars, I run into cousins I used to babysit. These little things don't add up to much when you consider that the tone of the village is the same. To this day, most people don't know what's going on up at the band office, and really don't care. Old people still sit by their windows looking out at the cars driving by, dogs running everywhere fertilizing the world. Home is home, what can you say?

It was winter again and I was back staying at my mother's when Aricka called. It was the first time I'd spoken with her in almost a year. Teenage romances are hardly binding thirteen years later. Especially when you're living in two different towns.

"Andrew, I hate calling you like this out of the blue, but I need your help." She still had that breathless quality about the way she talked. When we were young, I think it came from girlish enthusiasm, her brain working faster than her mouth, but now I fear it's from too many cigarettes.

"You sound serious, what's up?"

"It's anniversary time." I knew it was this week. You don't forget a thing like that, but I had long ago stopped being a part of her ritual.

"Yeah, I remember. I hear you still go out on the ice with those flowers of yours."

"Not this year. I'm pregnant, Andrew, and the doctor says I could deliver any time. He and Richard won't allow me to go out on the ice this year."

I almost dropped the phone is surprise. "Don't tell me you want me to go out there!"

She was quick to respond. "No, calm down Andrew. Richard offered but Ryan told him no. He wants to do it."

"But he never goes out on the lake, summer or winter."

"Well, he is this year. I don't feel right about it. It scares me. You know he's never been right about water since the accident. Something could happen out there."

I knew where this was leading. "Yeah, so?"

There was a deep breath on the other end. "Go with him, Andrew. Make sure everything's all right."

"Why me? You've got more cousins and relatives than you know what to do with. I don't want to sound rude, but why me?"

"I was thinking about that too," her voice got softer. "You brought Ryan out of whatever he was in, remember, in the hospital? And you went out with me that first time. I knew you didn't want to go, but you did. It has to be you, Andrew. Promise me you will?"

I was silent for a moment. Those feelings from thirteen years ago came back to the pit of my stomach. I was cornered.

"You win, I'll go." Aricka was ecstatic. She thanked me over and over again, but I barely heard her. I was thinking about how to handle this. I've found that, as you get older, your sense of courage tends to evaporate, disappears like the wind that blows across frozen lakes. I had promised I would go, but I wouldn't go alone. I immediately phoned up my buddy, my pal, William.

He was not pleased, even less than I was. "I don't even like the guy. It's your promise, you deal with it."

Luckily, the gods had allowed me to go to a hockey tournament a few months back with William. There we met these two girls from another Reserve and well.... Also, as the gods would allow it, I had the phone number of Marie, his long-suffering girlfriend. I casually mentioned this to William. You have to do these things with William, just to keep him in line. That's what friends are for.

He was flustered for a moment. "I'll tell Barb, then you'll be in trouble." I could hear the smile growing in his voice.

"I wasn't going out with Barb at the time. See you tomorrow at five. Bye." Before he could protest any more, I hung up.

I picked him up in my car the following day. He was glum, cranky and generally not impressed with me. "I hope you're happy." I was, sort of—as happy as I could be, under the circumstances. "Let's just get this over with." Good old William, overflowing with the milk of humanity.

We arrived at Ryan's house. It had changed little since that winter thirteen years before. Maybe a little more run down, but not much. Bachelors are like that. Ryan was already sitting on the porch, his hair blowing in the stiff wind, a bouquet of half frozen flowers on the porch beside him. You could tell he didn't want to do this, even from this distance, but he had to. Something inside was going to make him do it. It was necessary. Like going to the dentist.

"I really don't want to do this, Andrew" said William.

"Neither do I, but we gotta."

"My, aren't we plural these days?"

Once our car stopped in his driveway, Ryan got up and walked over, breath pouring out of his mouth like a little steam engine. I opened my window to talk to him.

"Hey Ryan, ready to go?"

Instead, he opened my door and motioned for me and William to get out. "Let's cut through the woods. It will be quicker than driving around to the lake, then walking. It's about half the distance."

William looked at me with worry. We would be following the same path Ryan took coming back from the accident. And we were going to the lake to remember the accident. This was becoming too much for William, almost too much for me. Ryan motioned for us to get out of the vehicle again and we did. I could hear William muttering under his breath, "You owe me big, Andrew."

"Well, let's go." Ryan closed the door behind me and started walking across his yard toward the woods a hundred feet distant. He quickly grabbed the flowers and nestled them in his arms. William and I followed along like ducklings behind their mother, every once in a while William giving me a shove to remind me that he was there at my insistence, (or my threat). Nobody said anything until we reached the lake.

I've never been one for ice fishing. I always found it too cold, and the fish were never tasty enough to warrant the numb extremities. Even still, I'd always find myself out on the lake for one reason or another at least once a year, same with William. But this was the first time for Ryan in all of these years, winter or summer. He had stopped walking just short of the ice. He looked out across the frozen expanse. I couldn't tell if he was working up nerve or lost in thought.

"It's been so long, I'm not sure where it was." His voice was almost lost in the rushing wind. "Aricka sort of gave me directions—a little off to the right of the spit she said." We all mentally found the spit and the direction. "That way, I guess."

Nobody moved. Again William was muttering: "Oh Marie, where are you? Your arms are so warm." February on our Reserve can make you very romantic.

Then suddenly Ryan was out on the ice, walking at a brisk pace. We were a good ten feet behind him before we started moving to catch up. Other than the wind, the only thing we could hear was the dry crunching of lake snow under our three sets of boots. We walked in a row, barely able to keep up with Ryan. There were old skidoo tracks all around us; it would have made walking a lot easier to follow them, but Ryan had his own course set.

Approximately half way to our destination, William finally said something aloud. "For God's sake, Ryan, slow down. My sweat is freezing".

Ryan stopped and looked around. "Oh, sorry. I wasn't thinking. Actually I was thinking too much"

"What's the hurry?" William looked miserable, his hands shoved way down deep in his pockets.

Ryan started to walk again. "No hurry, just lost in thought. It's all so familiar. Except it's not snowing."

Again William muttered to himself. "Give it time."

We were walking again, but not so fast. The shoreline was slowly drifting off behind us, and we were squinting now from the glare. William tightened his hood to keep the wind out. "Been a while, huh Ryan?"

Ryan looked like he wasn't listening, but he was.

"Yeah, a while." He kept walking. "You two didn't have to come with me you know. I could have handled it myself."

"I know, but your sister asked me as a favour. You know I could never say no to Aricka." That was true, even now, pregnant and all.

"I almost wish you hadn't come, Andrew. You make it more real. I remember the two of you at the hospital, then the crying. It's like I'm nine years old again."

The wind started to pick up and we soon found ourselves shouting three feet from each other. Another few minutes and we'd be there.

"You know, I always told people I really couldn't remember what went on that day, when they died. Actually I do, but I never wanted to talk about it. At the time I thought it was nobody's business, not even Aricka's. She wasn't there, she didn't see anything. Now I don't know."

We were approaching the channel, a couple hundred feet to the left was the other shore. The ice would still be quite safe, but it was like looking over the edge of a tall building: you knew you were safe, but....

"I was sitting in the back, the window was open. You remember how I used to get car sick. Dad was cursing about the snow, worried that he might be lost. Mom had just told me to roll the window up, it was too cold to have it open. That's when it happened. The car just lurched, dropped and I was thrown to the floor. Mom was screaming and I heard Dad call my name. Then I felt wet, and very cold. I climbed on the back seat, and saw water coming in my open window. I don't know if it was instinct or what, but I jumped through that window so fast it's all a blur."

William and I felt like we were being told a ghost story, in a very ghostly place, by a very ghostly person. It was not a warm feeling. I was beginning to wish Marie was there, too.

"I was only little then, so the ice could hold me up. I crawled across the broken ice to the solid stuff. It was cold, so damn cold, but it soon went away. I actually felt numb, then warm after awhile. All the time I could hear Mom and Dad behind me. They were trying to open their doors, but because of the water pressure, the doors wouldn't open."

"You don't have to tell us this." William said what I was thinking. I don't think Ryan heard, either because of the wind, or the memory.

"I remember sitting on the ice, crying. The water was up to the windows, and there were bubbles everywhere. It looked like it was boiling. Mom rolled down her window and tried to crawl through but she was kinda big. She wouldn't fit, I've never seen her try so hard at anything. She actually looked wedged in the window, then she reached for me, like she wanted me to pull her out, or maybe pull me in with her, I don't know. But the look on her face.... Then the car went under the water, with a large plopping sound. It wasn't there anymore. There were more bubbles, then her purse floated to the surface."

Ryan stopped both talking and walking. Evidently we had reached the spot, or as close to it as we were going to find, both in his memory and in our reality. He was looking down at the ice about six feet ahead of him.

"I just sat there for the longest time. I was nine years old, I didn't really know what was going on. I was scared, cold, in shock. After that it gets kind of blurry. I guess I found my way home."

Way over on the other side of the lake, I could see a car driving across the ice, heading to the Reserve. I wished I was in it.

"Is this why you've never been out on the lake since?"

"I guess. I just remember my Mom reaching for me. They're still out here you know. Somewhere below us. They never found the bodies."

William stamped his feet from both impatience and cold. "Can we get on with this please?"

"You're right. Let's get this over with." Ryan walked ahead a bit, then kneeled down and placed the flowers quietly on the ice. Then he started to stroke the flowers like Aricka had, like he was afraid to leave them. "Since the accident, I've always been afraid of this place. But Jesus, I'm twenty-two years old, I've got to stop being afraid at some point. In all this time I've never been able to say goodbye to them. After all, it's only water, right?

"Goodbye Dad. Goodbye Mom." He stood up and turned to face us, a slight smile on his face. "I was always Mom's favourite."

It was then he went through the ice. It all happened so quickly—a sharp cracking noise, Ryan looked down and then, like bread in a toaster, he slid straight down into the water, the ice buckling around the edge of the hole. A plume of water rushed up into the air, filling the space where Ryan had been a scant few seconds before, then falling onto the ice. Then there was silence. Even the sound of our breathing had stopped.

We stood there for a moment, not believing what we'd just seen. I remember instinctively racing for the hole and William grabbing me and wrestling me to the ground. I tried to crawl to the hole but he held me.

"Forget it, he's gone. He's under the ice somewhere, we'd never find him." He was right. There was no sign of him in the three-foot hole, just the occasional bubble.

"Come on man, let's just get the hell out of here. Tell the police." We stood up, I looked at the hole again, not knowing what to do. "Don't Andrew, let's go." William grabbed my arm and turned me towards home. We slowly headed back to the shore. William took one last look backwards. "Like he said, he always was his mother's favourite."

On the way back, it started to snow.

That was three days ago. Three long days ago. We told the police, and they went out with divers, but never found anything. I never thought they would. The community went into mourning, and the funeral was today. Even drunk I found it mildly amusing, them burying a body they never found.

Poor William. Fortunately or unfortunately, depending on how you look at it, he doesn't drink. From what I've heard, he hasn't come out of his house in the last few days—won't take calls either. The police had to practically threaten to arrest him if he didn't give them a statement.

And here I sit, waiting for the waitress to walk by so I can order another drink. I keep seeing Ryan disappearing into the ice, over and over and over again. I now have a new respect for alcoholics and why they drink. While I don't think this phase will last forever—I'm really a terrible alcoholic—it will hopefully last till I have new thoughts to think, and new memories.

I have just enough time to make last call. I manage to flag down the waitress as she passes. She nods at me.

"Yeah, yeah, I know. Double Rye and Coke. No ice."

Crisis Management

Angela was in one of her moods, which was rapidly turning me into one of my moods. Dodging people on the sidewalks of Peterborough, arguing at full power, is not an activity worthy of recommendation. Between the shoulders I accidentally bumped, the puddles I stepped in, and the concerned looks from strangers who seemed sure I was about to throw Angela through the nearest plate glass window, it was all I could do to keep up with my sister.

"You're wrong. You are absolutely, one hundred and ten percent wrong. That's why you're arguing with me. You know you're wrong but you refuse to admit it. Makes you fight all the harder, no matter how wrong you are. That's so like you." She said all that without giving me a single glance, the forceful gesticulations of her arms being the only obvious indication she was talking to me.

The reason we were walking through downtown Peterborough, and quarrelling, had the same origin. We had taken a cab from Trent University, where my sister takes an Ojibway language course while I hang out in the Native students' lounge picking up gossip, into the city to meet our mother. During the cab ride, we had started some small talk with the driver, who finally got around to noticing we were Native.

"God I envy you guys. Got land, no taxes, hunt and fish when you want, government takes care of all your problems. You people got it made."

I immediately felt Angela's body stiffen and her eyes focus in on the back of this poor guy's head. I grabbed her forearm and quickly whispered into her ear. "No, Angela." She shrugged my arm off saying "Yes, Andrew."

Using her best, polite, businesswoman voice that I knew

hid a formidable growing storm, she sat forward till her head was almost in the front seat. "Um, excuse me, sir, regarding your previous remarks concerning the favoured status of this country's Aboriginal people, I would just like to comment on that for a moment, if I may."

It was no moment, and no mere comment. In less than four minutes, maybe five if you count the rather colourful and earthy rebuttal from the cab driver, we found ourselves walking into Peterborough, having been dumped somewhere between the zoo and the downtown core. It seemed the cab driver did not appreciate Angela's take on his viewpoints.

I, on the other hand, had grown to know her indignant outbursts only too well. And they were becoming increasingly annoying and bothersome. I love my sister, and respect her opinions and would fight to the death for her, but I've always felt that there is a time and place to challenge the world. A cab on a cold fall day, a mile or two outside of town, is not one of them. And she knew it. Or should have.

"Goddamn Angela, let somebody else have an opinion, will you?"

She stopped in the street, glaring at me. "Don't tell me you agree with what he said?!"

"Of course not. Don't be silly. But what you just did, did nothing to change his opinion. In fact, you probably just created another negative view of Native people that he can share with his friends. That they are rude and like to pick fights. Sound familiar?"

"I wasn't going to let him think that he could just tell people things like that in his cab, like it was nothing. I believe in correcting these things, these stupid assumptions. If it was up to you, you'd let the whole world continue thinking and saying whatever they want about Native people. Not me. I am an Ojibway woman and I will have my people, and myself, spoken about with respect." She was breathing heavily at this point and people were making wide circles around us.

"It has nothing to do with that. I believe what you believe, but you have to know what fights to fight, and what battles to

either of those sound like a good idea to you?" He smiled a serious smile if I ever saw one. My sister met him smile for smile, except hers had that unmistakable subtext of having an ace up her sleeve.

"Go ahead. But first a few facts for your consideration. First of all, you used a derogatory epithet to describe one of your patrons, one which I can take you to court over. So already you've lost points. Two, I asked permission if I could touch that vest you seem so proud of. Therefore, it is difficult to prove assault when you have the assaultee's permission. Three, I am not being aggressive, argumentative, or violent. I have not even raised my voice. All I am asking for is an apology. Are the cops going to charge me for asking for a simple apology? Now, if you take it into that small head of yours to, as you say, break my arms off, you will be assaulting me. Any mark left on my arms by any act of aggression from you will stand up in a court of law as assault. How does that sound? In case you didn't notice, I'm a fourth-year law student."

Angela had lied. She planned community events for our Reserve. But I was sure impressed. I'm certain there were a dozen loopholes miles wide in what she said, but neither I nor the bouncer in a country bar were smart enough at the moment, under those immediate circumstances, to locate and exploit them. She made herself sound like the voice of authority and experience. I could see the wheels turning in the bouncer's head. Evidently what my sister had said sounded logical to him, too logical. He was trying to find a detour around her.

"Lady, you're crazy. Let go of me."

"That's not quite an apology. An apology starts with 'I'm sorry that—'"

"I'm not going to apologize to you. I didn't say nothing!" The big bouncer instinctively backed away from Angela, dragging her with him. He shouted to the bartender, a dozen or so feet away. "Hank, get Mickey. I've got a crazy woman here."

"Now, 'crazy woman' I don't mind as much as 'wagonburner.' 'Crazy woman' is a personal opinion, you of me. While 'wagonburner' is a broad reference to several million people across this continent. Very few of whom you probably know personally. It's like me saying all body-builders use steroids. Do you understand the difference?"

Again the bouncer's voice echoed across the smoke-filled "Saddle." "Mickey!"

An older man with a receding hairline came running up to us. He had on a white shirt with "The Saddle" logo on the pocket, worn jeans and, of course, cowboy boots to match the ensemble. Obviously he knew something was up but was trying to fully assess the situation. Bouncer man with Indian woman attached at the lapels. Second Indian man off to the side looking worried. The crowd watching. That pretty well summed it up.

"Hi, I'm Mickey Schultz, bar manager. Is there a problem here?"

Astonished, the bouncer looked at him. "For Christ's sake, Mickey, look." Pointing. "Her, get her off me. She won't let me go. Do something!"

A little perplexed, the bar manager stole a glance at my deceptively calm sister. It seems he was used to dealing with fights started by drunks, and various other predictable alcohol and bar altercations. But there stood my sister, calmly and almost serenely holding on to this big white man, who was definitely more agitated than she was.

Mickey cleared his throat. "Um, miss, could you please let go of my bouncer?"

"I really would like to. Really. But he has to apologize first. The minute he apologizes, we'll leave calmly. Honest Injun! Did you like that one, Vestboy?" She gave the bouncer a little shove, almost jokingly.

"Mickey!"

Mickey looked at me. "Who are you?"

"I sometimes wonder myself."

"He's my brother. But back to the issue at hand here, no

pun intended. This man made a racial slur against Aboriginal people. He used the term 'wagonburners.' I found it offensive and have since taken action, but I am willing to let bygones be bygones if he acknowledges the impropriety of that statement. Two words—"I'm sorry." That's all. I'm sure he has almost ten times that many words in his vocabulary. What do you say, Vestboy, ready yet?"

By this time a crowd had gathered, forsaking the dance floor for the show by the entrance. Mickey was conscious of this. Scratching his receding hairline, he tried to sound more authoritarian. "Tom, did you say that?"

Tom: "It was a joke. A joke. That's all. She's getting all excited over nothing. She's over-reacting. I've got nothing against Indians, you know that, Mickey. Get her off of me."

Angela: "Apologize."

Mickey: "Tom, maybe you should."

Tom: "Like hell. I told you I didn't say anything wrong. For the last time, it was a joke. If she can't take a goddamn joke, then let her deal with it. I'm not apologizing. She can stand here all night if that's what she wants. She's the one who's assaulting me."

For the first time in a long while, I made a suggestion. "Just an idea. Couldn't you make him apologize? I mean, you're his boss, aren't you?"

Mickey: "I don't have the authority. I just manage the bar. The owner's the one who hires and fires people."

Angela: "Get him."

Mickey: "Can't. He's in Florida for at least another three weeks."

Angela: "Feel like dancing like this for the next three weeks, Vestboy?"

Tom the bouncer looked into my sister's face. He was sizing her up again, not believing the fresh Hell she had introduced to his otherwise mundane life.

Tom: "Lady, if you had asked me nicely or maybe politely, I might have considered it. I'm nothing if not a gentleman. Besides, I'm supposed to be nice to the patrons. But when some nut case comes wandering in from the streets, into my place of work, and starts giving me orders and latching onto me like a tick or something, that's too much. Sorry, but I don't think she deserves an apology. Like I've said before and I'll say again, you are the one who's crazy, lady."

With perhaps her biggest and yet most sincere smile of the night, she responded proudly. "I am what I am." For some reason, I felt she had aimed that more at me than at Vestboy. Still smiling, Angela looked back to Micky. "I guess we have a Ojibway standoff here, huh?"

Mickey: "Don't you mean a Mexican standoff?"

Angela: "Not where we come from."

Mickey: "Look, can't we just sit down calmly and discuss this peacefully? Nobody wants any trouble here."

Angela: "Sure, get me a chair if you want. I'm not going anywhere. It's just as easy to hold Vestboy sitting as standing."

Mickey was thinking fast. "Well, that's a beginning." He pointed to the back of the bar, where a shaft of light pouring through the smoke peeked out of an open door. "Over there please, that's my office, and we'll sit down and discuss this. Sound good?"

"Sounds good to me," I added.

You could see the two of them weighing their options, and how to approach the situation without giving in. Somehow they agreed to the mediation, though not verbally. There was confirmation. "Lead on, Vestboy." There was a brief moment of awkward silence as both tried to figure out a way to move across the bar, attached the way they were. Being bigger, the bouncer made the first move, almost pulling Angela off her feet. She did her best to keep up and he, then Mickey made their way to the back of the bar. I brought up the rear, thinking.

It was the same old Angela, in the same predicament that I had grown to accept from her. Often in her zealousness to help our family, our community, or the whole Aboriginal nation, she was willing to face a den of lions. And, just as often, I was brought along for the ride. This particular situation was rapidly becoming a no win situation. It was apparent that neither my sister nor the bouncer had any intention of giving in. Which also meant that it was going to be a long night. On top of the immediate difficulty, this was exactly the type of predicament that could lose my sister her job with the band office. Band governments are notoriously shy of unwanted publicity, unless, of course, they orchestrate it themselves. And finally, our mother would be left waiting for us. Angela had inherited her formidable nature directly through the maternal gene.

They entered Mickey's office, a mess of paper and bottles of alcohol making up much of the decor. Angela and the bouncer shuffled in and off to one side to make room for the unattached. A quick survey of the room revealed only two chairs, one behind the desk, another in the corner, with part of the bracing broken off.

Mickey stated the obvious. "I think we need more chairs," and quickly left to rectify the problem. Wanting to be useful, I joined him to assist in the hunt. As I exited, I made a mental prayer that the two left in the room didn't kill each other during our brief absence.

In a few minutes we re-entered the room, each bearing a chair. Angela and the bouncer were still very much alive, though looking a little sheepish by this time. Evidently the adrenaline had worn off and the reality of the situation was finally dawning on them. I placed a chair behind Angela while Mickey did the same for Tom, the bouncer. After twisting their bodies in an effort to rest comfortably, they sat. Closing the door, Mickey took his seat. As usual, I got the broken one.

Mickey immediately took control of the meeting. Folding his hands almost in a prayer position, he started. "Tom, I want you to apologize."

The bouncer looked surprised. So did Angela. "I thought you didn't have the authority?"

"I'm taking the authority, in the absence of the owner. Our responsibility is to our patrons, to make their stay at "The

Saddle" enjoyable. I think it would be in everyone's best interest if we settled this problem here and now, and parted company. The most obvious way is with an apology."

The bouncer shook his head. "Sorry Mickey. No apology."

Mickey leaned back in his chair, thinking for a moment. "I see." He studied the two, then glanced at me. Suddenly, he stood up and approached the bouncer. "Tom, can I have a word with you privately?"

Tom and Angela looked at each other with a perplexed expression.

"How?"

"Good point. I'm sorry ma'am, your name is ...?"

"Angela." There was suspicion in her voice.

"Yes, Angela, could you move back as far as you can please. While still maintaining your contact with Tom, of course."

"Why?"

Mickey manoeuvred between them, making Angela involuntarily step back. "To give us a little privacy, please." Mickey patiently waited while Angela cautiously stepped backwards until her arms were perpendicular. They looked like a giant, ridiculous, letter H. Once she was far back as she could go, Mickey leaned up and whispered into Tom's ear. Sounding like air leaking from a tire, Mickey seemed to be lecturing Tom, and the expressions on Tom's face went from curiosity to anger, (which included a violent shaking of his head), to puzzlement and then finally to what appeared to be a certain understanding. As Mickey finished his clandestine conversation, the bouncer nodded in agreement.

Mickey turned to Angela. "Young lady, I believe Tom has something to say to you." He looked back expectantly at the bouncer.

Swallowing his pride with a large gulp, the bouncer faced Angela and said with a firm voice "I am sorry I called you a 'wagonburner.' There, happy?"

"No. More sincerity."

This time both Mickey and the bouncer, and admittedly even I, stared at her in surprise. To use an inappropriate metaphor, my sister has balls. Perhaps the proper metaphor is 'my sister sure has big ovaries.'

In our silence, she explained. "I don't believe you. Make me believe you." For a brief moment, we looked at each other, digesting her request with a certain amount of astonishment. Somewhere deep inside me, far from the pit of apprehension that appears during my sister's crusades, was a glowing furnace of pride in her.

Again Mickey cleared his throat. "Uhm, Tom, make her believe."

Clearly uncomfortable, actually fidgeting in his chair, Tom also cleared his throat. This was round two for the bouncer. "Okay. I am really, really, really sorry for calling you a 'wagonburner' and I promise it will never happen again. Will you please let go of my vest?"

Angela weighed the tone and honesty of the bouncer. We both knew the candour of that apology was probably as deep as the scarred and cracked varnish on the desk beside me, but I knew my sister believed that small battles were as important as big ones. Then, with a smile and an amused expulsion of breath through her nose, her fingers opened and my heart started beating again. Almost immediately Tom the bouncer backed away from her, putting as much distance as possible between them. You could see the eight distinct scratch marks on his leather vest clearly.

"I take it everybody's happy?" Mickey smiled.

Standing, Angela smoothed out her dress, an air of confidence and victory in every motion. "I am. Well, reasonably. We'll be leaving now. Let's go find Mom, Andrew." I opened the door for her and she was half-way outside when a sudden change of mind made her turn. She once again located the bouncer, saying quite distinctly, "the next time a Native person comes into this bar, I hope you'll remember me. Have a nice day." Imperiously, she exited, followed by me.

Once outside the bar, her demeanour fell and she let out the loudest victory cry I had heard since the All Ontario Indian Baseball Tournament two months before. She kept jumping up and down, slapping my shoulder in a glorious celebration of her conquest and success. The strain of the last half hour, though she hid it well, had been lifted and replaced by the knowledge that she had changed a little part of the world for the better.

"Let's celebrate."

"Sure, anything but a victory drink in another bar, please!"

Grabbing my arm, she dragged me off down the street. "I have a better idea. Chocolate sundaes, on me. The one with the bananas and everything. I'll even buy Mom one. You know I didn't think they'd give in. I had my worries there, but tenacity is my guardian spirit. The righteous always win. Are you paying attention? This is important."

No, I wasn't paying attention. I was too busy worrying about where I was going to borrow the fifty bucks I told Mickey I'd pay the bouncer to apologize to my sister, while we were getting the extra chairs. He had readily agreed to pass on my offer. When he whispered it to Tom in their moment of privacy, I had seen the bouncer shake his head until I caught, just barely, Mickey whispering something about an extra fifty dollars Mickey was willing to throw in just to end the situation. The price of pride had been established. It was one hundred dollars.

For me, fifty dollars was all it took to sell out my sister. My rationale was that she was not in an environment where she could or would win her particular battle. I wasn't sure it was a winnable or even that worthy a fight. Unlike the customs agent in New Jersey, Micky and Tom will likely remember my sister long after we left that bar. But had she really changed their minds? Probably not. Had she stayed there to the logical conclusion of the evening's events, whatever they would have been, would things have changed substantially in her or our people's favour? Would there have been a victory for her and her cause? Again, probably not. Still, the moral slogan, `either you're part of the problem, or part of the solution' reverberated loudly within my conscience, making me wonder if I had done the right thing.